I0682746

WINCHESTER LAW

CALIBER
BOOKS

Also from DOYLE TRENT

WINCHESTER LAW: Tales of the Old Wild West
Book Nine

Copyright 2025 Eagle One Media, Inc.
Original Copyright 1988 Doyle Trent
All Rights Reserved.

No part of this book may be copied or retransmitted without the express written permission of the publisher and copyright holder. Limited use of excerpts may be used for journalistic or review purposes. Any similarities to individuals either living or dead is purely coincidental and unintentional except where fair use laws apply.

For further information visit the Caliber Comics website:
www.calibercomics.com

Cover image by: Dubya2x

CHAPTER 1

The sound of gunfire reached his ears before he topped the sagebrush-covered hill. The Indian war cries, all too familiar, told him what was happening.

He had been riding alone for three days, riding a long-legged sorrel and leading four other horses, a pack horse carrying camp equipment, two Percherons with the harness on and another saddle horse.

Anyone could tell at a glance that he was a cattleman, with his lean body in a khaki shirt, black silk muffler hanging loosely around his neck, flat-brimmed sweat-stained hat and fringed shotgun chaps.

For three days he had seen no one, heard no one, only the westerly wind blowing through the sagebrush, waving the tall wheat grass. It was early July, and the sun bore down, turning his already sun-darkened face a shade darker.

The country around him was rolling hills, still green from the spring rains, but needing more rain.

At first he heard only small popping noises off in the distance, but he recognized the sound.

Then he heard the wild, crazy screams of Indians at war. He rode on with eyes nervously watching for danger, and when he approached a hill he knew it was the last barrier between him and the battle.

Dismounting, he left his five horses under the crest of the hill and crawled on his knees, carrying his rifle. At the top, he lay on his

5

belly, looked out onto a grassy yucca plain and watched the attack on a wagon train a quarter mile away.

Eleven wagons. They hadn't had time to swing them in a circle, and the wagons were bunched up in a straight line. Somehow they had managed to get the horses unhitched and tied to the wagon wheels.

With pale blue eyes, wrinkled at the outer edges from years of squinting across the wide plains of Texas, he counted twelve men and a few women and children, all lying under the wagons. They were firing as fast as they could, but most of the men were firing muzzle loaders, and had to ramrod the powder and lead in, while the Indians had the faster breech loading rifles.

Still, the fire from under the wagons was taking its toll. He counted four bodies scattered beyond the wagons, and four horses down. He couldn't tell how many of the whites had been hit.

It was easy to guess what had happened. The Indians had swept down on the wagons from a bluff to the south, and when the return fire got too heavy and they had to reload, they just retreated to the bluff, reloaded, regrouped and attacked again. It was late afternoon, and he guessed that just before dark the big attack would come. The whites were outnumbered five to one. They would be overrun.

He lay on the hill north of the battle and tried to figure out what to do. If he could join them, he would be a valuable ally with his new Winchester repeating rifle. But the Indians would see him coming and they would concentrate their fire on him to keep him away from the wagons. He wouldn't have much of a chance.

Well, he couldn't just lie there on his belly and watch a wagon train wiped out and men, women and children murdered. The Indians would kill them all. After fighting the Comanche down south in Texas, he knew what the Indians would do. Any poor white-eyes who were taken alive would die a slow agonizing death when the savages got him back to their camp. Torturing prisoners of war was a favorite recreation in the Comanche camps.

He had to do something.

Below him in the valley the firing continued. And the hysterical screams of the savages, riding bareback on good horses that had to have been stolen, sometimes carried farther than the sound of gunshots.

What to do? He could ride for help, but he was a stranger in that territory, and he didn't know where the nearest help was. He figured he was somewhere east of the settlement called Colorado City, but he didn't know how far east. Help could be too far away. While he was trying to decide what to do, the decision was made for him. He looked back at his five horses in time to see their heads come up, see them look to the east. He saw the two savages at the same time they saw him.

They were nearly naked and they too rode bareback with nothing more than a leather thong looped in their ponies' mouths to control them. Their faces were painted in loud colors with a crazy design, and their long black hair was pulled behind their ears and tied with red rags. They carried long-barreled breech loading rifles.

Immediately they dropped off their ponies, and one of them let out an ear-splitting scream that could be heard clear across the valley.

The young white man reacted just as fast. His Winchester was already loaded and cocked, and he rolled onto his back, glanced down the barrel and squeezed the trigger. A savage yell was cut off as an Indian dropped with a .44 slug in his chest. But the other red man had his rifle to his shoulder and fired hastily. A rifle slug hit the ground beside the white man. A near miss.

In a second, the white man had another cartridge levered into the firing chamber of his Winchester and in another second he fired again. The recoil slammed his right shoulder like a hammer as he fired while still on his back. The bullet hit where he aimed, and that battle was over.

But not the danger.

The shots were heard in the valley below, and firing there ceased as everyone, including the attackers, looked up the hill toward him. He was seen. They would be coming. He had to ride for it. Ride like hell.

In four running steps he was at the side of his half-thoroughbred saddle horse, and then he was in the saddle, wrapping the lead rope around the saddle horn. Spurring hard, he got his horses into a gallop down the hill toward the wagons. His string of horses were tied head to tail. They had been led that way for more than a hundred miles, and they pulled back very little as he got the whole string into a dead run down the hill.

What he feared would happen was happening. The Indians were concentrating their fire at him, and some were riding toward him. He held the rifle and reins in his left hand and drew his six-shooter, an old percussion gun that had been converted to fire metallic cartridges. He had his horses running as hard as they could run, jumping the sagebrush, dodging the yucca, jumping the shallow gullies.

He fired at a painted face, and saw it disappear. At another. They were coming closer. Then the men under the wagons were shooting, trying to cover his advance. Three of them crawled out from under the wagons and kneeled on one knee for better aim. Another savage fell from his horse. The young white man let out a wild rebel yell himself as he rode for his life, firing his six-shooter. Now he was at the wagons and he headed for a break between the second and third wagons. His horses jumped over a wagon tongue and he was on the other side, stepping down from the saddle before his horses came to a complete stop.

There was no time to say howdy, nor look around. He hit the ground on his belly again with the Winchester in his hands. He aimed, fired, levered in another cartridge, fired again. A man beside him fired, then reloaded his rifle from the muzzle. The young man with the Winchester repeating rifle fired several more shots as fast as he could aim and lever in more shells.

The Indians were circling the wagons now, shooting from all directions. They wore a mixture of Indian and white men's clothes. One had a fedora on his head and another wore a black stovepipe hat. Most were bare-chested, but a few wore white men's cotton shirts. Another wore a white man's wool pants. The young man turned around and fired in the opposite direction. When the hammer of his gun clicked harmlessly, he ran to his pack horse, reached inside a canvas pannier and pulled out a box of cartridges. He lay flat but held the rifle to his shoulder as he shoved the cartridges into its side. Twice, he stopped reloading long enough to fire single shots, then resumed feeding the cartridges until he had the magazine filled.

Now the shooting was tapering off. The savages were no longer yelling. A lone, earsplitting, high-pitched, wavering yell came from the Indians, and the shooting stopped. The attackers rode at a gallop back to the bluff out of rifle range.

It was quiet. Deathly quiet. Until someone said, "They're hightailin' it."

The young man stood and looked around. He saw a ragtag assortment of people. Men in bib overalls and lace-up, high top shoes. Women in long cotton dresses, also wearing high top shoes. Five children, two girls and three boys from five years old to about twelve. One man was on his side with his knees drawn up. Another was flat on his back, not moving. A woman knelt over him and cried silently.

"Joel." The speaker's voice was trembling. "Think they'll come back, Joel?"

The man addressed was carrying a better gun than the rest, a Spencer carbine that loaded itself from a magazine in the butt stock when he opened and reclosed the breech. He took his time answering. He was short and wiry, with a buckskin shirt, black in spots with age, and a wide-brimmed floppy hat. His faded colorless eyes took in the men, women and children then gazed out over the yucca flats. He seemed to be mentally counting the bodies out there. Six or eight. "Don't think so," he said, finally.

The wounded man who had been lying on his side was now on his back with two women working over him. They had his shirt off and were daubing blood from a wound in his right shoulder. Another woman knelt beside the dead man and closed his eyes with her fingertips. She put an arm around the new widow. "He's with the Lord now."

A pitiable wail came from the widow. "No-o-o. I can't let him go." Two other women came up and tried to console her.

Joel approached the newcomer and held out his hand to shake. "I'm Joel Hoskins, wagon master. I'm mighty glad you come along. They was givin' us fits. That repeatin' rifle of yours made a lot of difference."

The young man shook with him. "Name's Williams. William C. Williams. Youall saved my bacon too." He talked with a drawl. "Seems to me they gave up easy."

"We made it tough for 'em. And they prob'ly didn't want to waste any more ammunition and any more braves on us. Where was you headin' for, Mr. Williams?"

"Bill. Most folks call me Bill. I just came down from Wyoming. I left a hundred and fifty cows and some bulls down here."

"You from Wyomin'?"

Bill Williams had to grin at that. "Not hardly. I'm from Texas. Came through here about a month ago with three thousand Texas longhorns, heading for a buyer at Laramie. This looks like good grass country, and I cut out a hundred and fifty cows and twelve bulls, figuring to come back and take up a homestead."

"Good cattle country, all right. Lots of grass now that they've killed off the buffalo."

"You folks heading for Denver? Or Colorado City?"

"Colorado City. These people are farmers. Come from Wichita. Land's still free out here. There's some good crop soil over there under them rocky hills." Joel nodded to the west where the jagged tops of the purple mountains were barely visible against the skyline.

"I've been warned that the Indians around here are none too friendly. What breed are they?"

"Cheyenne, mostly. Some Arapahos."

"Is somebody selling them guns?"

Joel snorted, "Huh." His features pulled tight in anger. "The U.S. government gives 'em guns. Feels guilty about killin' off the buffalo and tries to make up for it by givin' the redskins guns to hunt with. Hunt, hell. The only thing they hunt is white men's stock. And white men's scalps."

Their conversation was interrupted by a man in denim overalls. "Air we agoin' on tonight, Mr. Hoskins?"

"Yep." Joel turned on his heels. "We got wounded to get to a doctor. How many horses did we lose?"

"Lost two. Might haveta leave a wagon behind."

"I've got two harness horses," Bill Williams said. "You can hitch them up. I'll go along with you to Colorado City. Need to buy some stuff anyway."

He helped strip the harness off a dead horse and another that was shot in the left side. Once the harness was off the wounded horse, its owner led it away a short distance, then shot it between the eyes. He walked back, scowling. "He was hurtin'," he muttered. "Couldn't of lived more'n a few hours."

The man's wife looked at Bill Williams with pain in her eyes. "Mr. Williams—I overheard you say that was your name—we surely are obliged to you for lettin' us use one of your horses."

Bill shoved his flat brimmed hat back, showing thick brown hair, and grinned a wry grin. "I don't know how I got here without getting at least one of my horses shot. Go right ahead. The bay with socks on his hind feet works the off side. The other is the nigh horse."

Both his Percherons were hitched up to replace the dead horses, and the wagon train got moving again. The Indians had disappeared. Joel Hoskins, riding a red roan with a roman nose, left first and stayed a half mile ahead of the wagons, watching for danger and picking out the route. There was no road, only a dim trail. Bill caught up with him, and they rode side by side, their horses stepping around the tough, jagged yucca.

"You're gonna homestead somewhere around here, you say?"

"Yep. We—my brothers and I—need more grass, and this looks like a mighty good territory."

"I hear there's big money in cattle."

"There is in some parts of the country if you've got the grass. And as far as I can see here the grass is stirrup high."

"It is, and it's all free. But," Joel Hoskins shot him a sideways glance, "there's the damned Injuns. Damned savages make livin' here a dangerous proposition. A man alone ain't got a chance."

"Yeah." Bill Williams studied the country ahead, then squinted to the north and to the south. He half-expected to see an Indian on every hill, watching them. "But a man's got to take a chance now and then."

He carried the Winchester across the front of the saddle, and he kept his finger close to the trigger.

CHAPTER 2

It turned dark, and the horses were tiring. Men were using long whips to keep them going.

"Hate to treat 'em that way," Joel Hoskins said, "but we can't be far from the settlement now. We'll come to a better road purty soon and that'll make it easier on the horses."

They went on. The wagons bounced over the sagebrush until they joined a road that came from the north. The road was nothing more than two tracks, but the tracks were fairly smooth and the traveling was easier. No more bouncing, and no more jerking on the collars of the harness horses.

Joel had been staying well ahead of the wagons, and now he turned his horse around and rode back. Bill Williams went with him.

"How far are we agoin' tonight, Mr. Hoskins?" a woman asked.

"We're gonna see the lights of Colorado City any minute now," he answered. "When we get there, we can let these animals rest."

"They cain't go much further," a man said.

Only a dim outline of the wagons and horses could be seen, and the voices came out of the dark. Bill could see that his pack horse and the other saddle horse were leading well tied behind a wagon.

Soon the night turned so black that the humans couldn't see the road, but the horses could, and they instinctively followed it. Bill and Joel Hoskins rode into a wide sandy draw with the wagons behind them. When they rode out of the draw they saw lights ahead. Dim lights, but definitely man-made lights.

"There she is," Joel said. "There's our destination." He turned in his saddle and hollered back. "We're there, folks. That's Colorado City."

A woman's voice came out of the dark, "Thank the Lord."

"Did you hear that, Mabel?" a man's voice said. "See them lights. We're here."

"How long have you been traveling?" Bill asked. "Seventy-two days. Had to stop every few days and let the horses rest and graze a day or two. These folks need their horses, and they wanted to keep 'em in good shape."

"Can't do any farming without horses," Bill allowed. "Can't do much of anything without horses."

Gradually the lights came closer, but still they saw no other sign of life. Only the dim lantern lights.

"Must be close to midnight," Joel mused. "Prob'ly ever'body's in bed."

They traveled on, wagon wheels creaking, until a huge black wall, blacker than the night, loomed before them.

"Looks like a pole fence," Bill allowed.

"Fence, hell. That's a stockade. These people must be afraid of the Injuns too." Joel reined up. The horses pulling the lead wagon stopped behind him. Then all the wagons stopped.

"Hello-o-o!" Hoskins yelled. He yelled again, "Hello-o-o-o!"

A voice came from the direction of the wall. "Who's there?"

"We're travelers," Hoskins yelled. "We got eleven wagons. We were hit by the Injuns back east a ways and we got one dead and two wounded."

"Where'd you come from?"

"Wichita, Kansas. My name is Joel Hoskins. These people hired me to guide 'em to Colorado City. Is this Colorado City?"

"This is her. We're gonna open the gate. Come on in."

Gate hinges squeaked and lantern lights bobbed in the dark. "Come on in," a man's voice hollered.

Joel Hoskins turned in his saddle again. "Let's go, folks. Looks like they're forted up."

Hoskins and Bill Williams led the way and the wagons followed. When they got closer, men holding lanterns lighted the way to the gate and through it. Inside, Bill guessed from the distance between lights that the stockade surrounded about an acre and a half. There was a two-story hotel made of rough lumber and a few tents. Horses stood inside. The stockade walls were made of shoulder high pine timbers with the bark on. Men stood guard, looking over the wall into the darkness outside.

"Pull your wagons over here," a man said, using his lantern to show the way. The wagons followed him until all eleven of them were stopped along the west side.

"You can unhitch here."

"Is there any feed for the horses?" Joel Hoskins asked, pulling the saddle off his red roan.

"Not a bit. We have to turn 'em out in the daylight and let 'em graze. Kinda dangerous, but we have to let 'em graze."

Bill Williams squinted at the man carrying the lantern, trying to read his features in the dark. All he could see was a bearded man, average height, wearing a wide-brimmed hat.

"Had a lot of trouble with the Indians, huh?"

"A powerful lot of trouble. Too many stockmen and their families murdered. Almost ever'body in El Paso County is in here now."

"Have you got supplies?"

"Yeah, we got enough for a while. Fifteen wagons came down from Denver day before yesterday with about fifty soldiers. The soldier boys went back to Denver, howsomever."

"You're not getting any help from the army, then?"

"None. We asked. The governor sends messages to the general gover'ment in Washington, but nothin' comes of it."

Bill Williams off-saddled his horse and unloaded his pack horse. He turned them loose with the other horses in the stockade, then went back to the man with a lantern. "My name is Williams. My brothers and I raise beef on the edge of the Llano Estacado in Texas, and we have to fight off the Comanche now and then. Somebody gets killed every once in a while. But we never had to hole up like this."

"Well, I'll tell you somethin', mister, we ain't agoin' to live this way much longer. There's almost enough men and guns here to take the fight to the Indians, and if we don't get any help from the army, we're agoin' to put a stop to this ourselves."

"We tried to do that a couple of times, but there's so much territory where white men have never been that we couldn't find them."

"We find 'em, and when we do that'll be the end of 'em. You're from Texas, you say?"

"Yeah. I aim to take up a homestead on the plains over east. Is there a land office here?"

"There is. Well, I got to git up there and keep my eyes peeled. Nobody's been hurt by an Injun at night, but we have to keep a watch anyways."

"I was told that Colorado City is a good-sized town. Is there a town out there?"

"There is, but most stuff worth stealin' is in here." The man walked away, shaking his head and muttering, "We ain't agoin' to live this way much longer."

The new arrivals were bedded down by now, some in their wagons and some under the wagons. Their horses had been turned loose to mix with the other horses inside the stockade. Bill Williams picked a spot between a wagon and the stockade wall, unrolled his tarp-covered bed, pulled off his boots and crawled between the blankets.

He lay awake for an hour or more, wondering whether he'd done something dumb by cutting out a hundred and fifty cows and planning to homestead here. When his mother and dad were killed by a Texas tornado, he and his two brothers tried to keep the Running W in the black. But they needed more land. Grass was short in Texas and it took a good seventy-five acres to graze a cow and calf the year around. When they heard that some of their neighbors were getting a trail herd together to take to Wyoming, they'd rounded up eight hundred and fifty of their own.

Bill, the middle brother, had gone with the trail herd and collected the money for the Running W cattle. But he had another goal: to look for a territory where cattle could be grazed on the public domain for nothing and where he could claim a hundred and sixty acres for himself.

Hell, he'd allowed, if those northerners could buy Texas cattle for seven dollars a head, graze them on free grass a year and sell them for fifteen dollars, why couldn't he do the same? Only, being a Texan he knew he wouldn't like the cold and snow of Wyoming and Montana, and when they'd passed through Colorado on the Dawson Trail, he figured that was a good territory. Especially with a railroad coming to Denver. That was the rumor, anyway. He'd come back.

Now, with the Indians on the warpath, killing every white-eye they could get in their gunsights, he wondered about that plan.

Not that he hated Indians. He had every reason to hate them, but he didn't. Hell, if he were an Indian he'd be fighting mad too at the way the buffalo hunters had killed off their livelihood. Taking the hides and tongues and leaving the rest to rot. Hell, the buffalo was the Indians' bread and butter, clothing and shelter and even weapons. Without the buffalo, they had to steal white men's beef to survive.

Nope, he couldn't blame the Indians for being fighting mad. But dammit the white man had to live too, and when a man sees the mutilated bodies of his hard working neighbors killed by Indians, he can't help but get fighting mad himself.

Damn. Bill Williams lay on his back, pulled his hat over his eyes, and tried to get some sleep.

CHAPTER 3

The whole camp was up by daylight. Someone yelled that the Anway Hotel was serving hotcakes, bacon and coffee for twenty cents a plate. Bill Williams washed his face in a sheet metal stocktank and shaved, using a straight razor and a mirror hanging from the fence. He combed his brown hair straight back, then hotfooted it over to the hotel. His spurs with wagon wheel rowels made muffled ringing sounds as he walked.

Everyone ate at a long wooden table while four women carried plates of food and tin cups of coffee from the kitchen. Bill counted eighteen men, six women and six children at the table. Outside, other women had built fires and were cooking breakfast for their families.

"I'm takin' my animals out to graze," said a man wearing baggy wool pants and a muslin shirt with no collar, "and I'm gonna see to my oats."

"We're takin' all the horses out," said another. "We're all goin'. There's enough of us that them Injuns'll keep their distance."

"I'll go with you," said Bill Williams. "I've got five horses. I'll keep my saddle and bridle on one I know I can catch and turn them all loose to graze."

"Is that one of them new Winchester repeatin' rifles you got?"

"Yeah. I bought it at Santa Fe last April, just before we started up the Dawson Trail."

"What'll you take for it?"

Bill Williams shook his head. "I need that gun."

17

"What kind of pistol you got?"

"It was made in Texas by Dance Brothers and Park. I had it fixed to fire .44 caliber metal cartridges, the same as my Winchester."

"You're well-armed. Most of us are still shootin paper cartridges, the kind you have to bite the end off from."

"Is it true, what someone said, about the general government giving guns to the Indians?"

"That's the rights of it. The government tried to make gentlemen farmers out of 'em. Gave 'em flour, sugar, beans and even some cattle. The deal was, the Cheyenne were supposed to stay in their territory on Sand Creek and leave us alone, but some of them young bucks got restless and went back to their old ways."

"Trouble is, this territory ain't a state and we got no one in Congress except a delegate who ain't allowed to vote, and the U.S. government don't give a hoot about us."

"We shot the hell—excuse me, ma'am—out of them Injuns at Sand Creek a couple a years ago, and some of them senators who never saw an Injun in their lives think we ought to be ashamed of ourselves."

"I was there. They accused us of killin' women and children, but at two or three hundred yards you can't tell a buck from a squaw."

"You from Texas, Mister?"

"Yeah," Bill Williams answered after swallowing a mouthful of bacon. "I'm planning to homestead somewhere east of here."

"You'll have to go a way east. All the land up and down Monument Creek's been claimed. There's crops growin'."

"I'm no farmer. Growing cattle is all I know."

"You'll have to pick a spot the Ladder ain't already claimed. And that Dutchman's got most of the good water."

"Who?" Bill stopped chewing and his head came up. This was something he hadn't heard of.

"Old Aarnstadt. Him and his Eastern conglomerate. They brought a lot of cattle from Kansas and the Indian Nation, and they built a house and a barn and some cattle pens on Owl Creek. I'd cal'clate they've got over four thousand cattle grazin' on the public domain."

"Yeah, he's got about a dozen riders and they're all carryin' repeatin' rifles like yours, and the Injuns ain't about to take them on."

"Well now." Bill put down his knife and fork and wiped his mouth with the back of his hand. "I just came down from Wyoming, and I didn't see one cow brute. Not even my own. And I didn't see any grass that looked like it had been cropped. Not this year, anyhow. So there's got to be a lot of territory that hasn't been preempted."

"Well," the bearded man stood and slapped a floppy hat on his head. "I've got some stock to see to."

"Me too," another man said, standing.

Within one minute, the room had been cleared of men, and the women began gathering dirty dishes.

Bill Williams stayed three days in Colorado City. He was surprised to see that the town was well-developed, with everything a town was supposed to have. Even a red-lantern district. Colorado Street was alive with traffic: wagons, buggies and horseback riders, but everyone was looking out beyond the buildings, watching for Indians. Every other business on the street was a saloon. There was no courthouse, though Colorado City was the county seat of El Paso County. There was a jail made of thick timbers hauled down from the mountains to the west, but it was empty. There was an elected county sheriff and some county commissioners, but they had no offices. To the southwest, looming over everything, was the fourteen thousand-foot mountain called Pikes Peak. Beyond the mountain, men were desperately searching for gold. Most of the town's men refused to stay in the stockade, but they sent their women and children there, and every man kept a gun handy. It was understood that if anyone was attacked, the whole town would come to the rescue.

There was a U.S. Land Office in town, but the door was locked. Bill tried the door morning and evening, but never saw anyone there.

"He's got a place over by the Soda Springs," Bill was told. "That's where he stays most of the time."

"Well, hell, how does anybody get hold of him?"

"They don't, 'til he's ready to be got hold of."

"Gets paid by the general government, but they don't know what he's doin'. Or not doin'."

"Well." Bill scratched his jaw and looked down at the plank sidewalk. "I haven't got a spot picked out to file on anyway. But," he looked up and gazed eastward, "I will have, and when I do I'll have to find that jasper."

His next task was to write a letter to his brothers. He mailed it at the Colorado City post office. There wasn't much to say, just that he was planning to buy a wagon and some supplies and hunt for a place to stake a claim. He'd already sent them a certified check from Cheyenne for the Running W cattle he'd sold in Wyoming.

He bought what he thought he'd need, a light spring wagon, some rough lumber from a sawmill on the west side near the Soda Springs, three rolls of tarpaper, three hundred rods of smooth galvanized wire, a small, sheet-metal stove, some building tools and some groceries.

"Ain't seen nor heard of an Injun for a couple days now," a bearded townsman said, "but they're out there. If they see you, you'd better be right with your Maker."

Grinning a wry grin, Bill said, "I hope to keep my scalp, but I can't raise beef from town. I've got cattle running wild out there, probably scattered plumb to Kansas."

With his Percherons hitched to the wagon and his saddle horses tied behind, he gathered the lines, climbed up to the spring seat, clucked to his team and left town. As he left, he took one quick glance back, then kept his eyes constantly searching the empty country around him. After he had gone five miles, he realized he was alone again in a dangerous and hostile land, a land where a man's life, especially a stranger's life, was worth nothing.

After four hours of bouncing over the clump grass, dipping in and out of the draws and going around dry creek beds, he began looking for water. A cow could go a long way for water, but she had to have it. Grass was plentiful and free, but water wasn't so plentiful.

To the south, the land was flat, almost as flat as the Llano Estacado, and to the north the country rolled over small, low hills toward a line of distant dark blue trees. He had heard about the pine forests northeast of Colorado City. Cold. The temperature there was always a good ten degrees colder than down on the plains. Felt good in July and August, but a harsh, cruel climate in the winter. The snow was deep there in the winter, as deep as in the mountains, burying the grass. Not the place to stake a claim.

When the sun was almost straight up, he stopped, unhitched the team and let the horses graze while he ate cold bread and bacon. He stood on the wagon seat and studied the country around him. There had to be water somewhere. Was that a bunch of trees way over there, over to the southeast? Yes, it looked like trees. Where there were trees there might be water.

He hitched up the team again and turned them southeast. His eyes were busy, watching for cattle.

And Indians.

It took an hour to get there, and when he did he was disappointed. There had been water, but the creek bed was nothing but mud now. He believed that if he dug a hole in the bed he would strike water, but he couldn't dig enough holes to water a hundred and fifty cattle. In the spring when the snow melted or when it rained, the creek held water. But not now.

He turned his horses north, off the yucca flats, toward the rolling blue-green hills. An hour later his team was pulling hard to get the wagon over a hill, and two hours later he spotted another line of trees. North and west. He turned toward the trees, went another mile and spotted cattle off in the distance. Twenty-two cows and a bull.

Right then Bill Williams wanted to do two things. He wanted to see if there was a stream up there among those trees, and he wanted to look at the cattle, see if they were his. He couldn't do both before dark.

Well, he decided, the cattle would still be somewhere near here in the morning, and after seeing them, he would have been willing to bet there was a creek up there. The cattle had to water somewhere. Clucking to his team, he went on, the wagon bouncing and rattling

When he got closer, his heart beat faster. Cottonwoods. Big healthy ones. "Come on, old ponies," he said to his horses, "maybe we've found a home." He was excited. But he was wary.

Indians needed water too.

CHAPTER 4

It was a creek, all right. Only about four feet wide, but the sandy bottom land and the steep cutbank on the north side told him the water had been a hell of a lot higher and swifter at times. That and the driftwood piled up in places. Leafy cottonwoods rose a good seventy-five feet. Their shade created a cool pleasant glen along the creek. The grass on the south side, on the floodplain, grew higher and greener than the buffalo grass farther out on the plains. Blue grass, he guessed. Good stock feed.

Night was coming on. He had to get his horses watered and hobbled, and he wouldn't have much time to explore. He unhitched his Percherons, pulled the harness off, and led all five horses to the creek. After they drank their fill he hobbled all but one of the saddle horses, using soft gunny sacks to hobble the front feet and soft cotton rope to sideline a hind foot to a front foot of each horse. A saddle horse, one he knew he could trust, was picketed on a thirty-foot rope. He wanted to keep at least one horse close where he knew he could find him in the dark if necessary.

With only a little daylight left, he walked up the creek to a place where he could climb the cutbank. There, he took a long careful look around. A small herd of antelope grazed two hundred yards to the north. And farther to the north, probably fifteen miles, was the pine forest.

This looked like a good spot, a place to camp and a place to live. He slid down the bank on the seat of his pants, walked upstream a way. Suddenly, he stopped. Someone else had thought it was a good spot too. Just ahead back among the cottonwoods were the remains of a camp fire.

He squatted and picked up a handful of ashes. They were old and dry, and the charcoal crumbled in his fingers. Whoever had camped here hadn't done it recently. Maybe not even this year. But someone knew about this spot. The Cheyenne? If they were prowling this part of the country, they might come back.

His supper was cold, but until he'd done some exploring and knew more about the territory, he was afraid to build a fire. He unrolled his bed under the trees and surrounded it with driftwood, hoping that would keep anyone from sneaking up on him. With his boots under the tarp at the foot of the bed and his six-gun under the blankets with him, he lay on his back and listened to the cottonwood leaves rustle in the breeze. A pleasant spot. He hadn't even seen any rattlesnakes. A very pleasant spot. And it was free.

Well, not exactly. People had been killed trying to homestead in the west. If he wasn't killed, he would at least be in constant danger. Nope. If he lived here the required five years and proved up on his claim, he would have earned it.

Nothing was really free.

At first light he pushed the blankets down and pulled on his boots. Nothing moved. There was no sound at all. Only a pale light shone through the trees, not enough to make a shadow. He sat still, listening. No sound at all. Were his horses still there? He knew a Comanche could see in the dark, move in the dark, and smell horses and white-eyes. He knew how they liked to steal horses. The Cheyenne were no different.

Standing, he holstered the six-gun on his left hip, butt forward, and picked up the rifle. Stepping over the driftwood, he walked out from under the trees, trying to be quiet. He ought to take his spurs off. A cowman never took his spurs off his boots. But it was impossible to walk quietly with spurs on, and he knew he ought to take them off now.

Instead, he walked slowly, carefully, watching each step until he was away from the trees and could see out onto the plains. The horses were there. The hobbled ones had moved about a hundred yards, but his sorrel saddle horse was right where he'd left him. All were grazing peacefully. It was a good time of day for grazing, before the sun heated up the air and the flies got bad.

Grinning with relief, he went to his wagon, sliced some bacon and built a fire out of driftwood. While the bacon sizzled, he washed his face in the creek and combed his hair with a metal comb he'd carried in one of his panniers. No use looking like one of the savages. He unwrapped some of the bakery bread he'd bought and ate breakfast. Then he collected his horses and led them to water.

When the sun came up, so did the birds. Meadowlarks. They sang their song over and over. He liked hearing them sing. A beautiful morning and a beautiful spot. Too bad his brothers weren't there.

Soon after sunup he was horseback, riding his long-legged sorrel. He headed south, looking for the cattle he'd seen the day before. Always, his eyes were busy, watching the horizon, every hollow in the earth, every bush. He could see where the cattle had grazed, and he saw the cattle droppings. When he topped a low hill, he saw the cattle.

They were wild, but he got close enough to read the brands. His Running W was barely visible under the animal hair, but the road brand, the big H burned on the side of each head of cattle that came up the Dawson Trail, was easy to see. Twenty-four cattle were here. Where were the other hundred and twenty-six? Make that a hundred and thirty-six counting the bulls.

The sun was high now, and the heat was bearing down on him. He pushed his hat back and wiped sweat from his forehead with a shirtsleeve. When he went on, he rode in a wide circle. Just before noon he found another bunch, thirty-four, all wearing the big H. Wishing he'd made a sandwich out of the bread and bacon, he rode on, across dry washes, wide grassy draws, over hills. White clouds began gathering on the western horizon, and he wished they would gather overhead and shield him from the relentless sun. After another hour he found forty more cows and six of his bulls.

"You old boys ought to socialize more," he said aloud. "You're ganging up on this bunch of cows." An hour later he turned back toward his camp, and soon crossed a cattle trail, which probably went to the creek farther upstream from where he'd spent the night. Those

Texas longhorns could smell water miles away, and that creek had to have come out of the mountains or out of the pine forest. It had to be a long creek, snaking its way across the plains to a river somewhere, most likely the Arkansas.

Out of curiosity, he turned his horse and followed the trail. It was well used, and the cattle that had started it knew where they were going. Sure enough, by mid-afternoon the trail led him to the creek, to a place where the stream was wider, but shallow, where there were no trees and no sandy creek bottom. There were more cattle. A strange-looking breed, shorter legs, shorter horns, and carrying more beef. Not his cattle.

Nor were they wild. They lay and stood by the creek chewing their cuds when he rode up to them and looked them over. No road brand. Instead a brand that looked like two parallel lines and...then he remembered. These cattle belonged to an outfit called the Ladder. An outfit belonging to an Eastern conglomerate.

Was he in Ladder territory, on land they had preempted? He wondered if the Ladder outfit was friendly.

He turned his horse back toward his camp, wondering too if he was going to find himself in the middle of a range war.

As well as an Indian war.

Before approaching his wagon, he rode all around it, looking for sign of a visit from humans. His horses were still there, hobbled. He would have to build a fence of some kind of keep the horses from wandering away. Let's see, he had the cutbank on one side, and a fence could be built of driftwood on another side. The galvanized wire he'd brought would have to do for the other two sides. The blue grass along the creek would feed five horses for a while, but just how long, he would have to learn from experience. Eventually the fence would have to be moved to surround more grass.

Cooking over a fire was taking a chance, but cold meals couldn't be endured forever. He bedded down away from the fire, back under the trees in the darkest spot he could find. Lying awake with his guns handy, he listened, and every little sound he couldn't immediately identify set his nerves on edge, his ears straining. Finally, from exhaustion, he slept.

Building a fence for a horse pasture was the first thing he had to do, even before building a shelter for himself, and, after taking a walk around, he set to work on it. His saddle remained on a bay horse, ready to ride for it if need be. At times, he used the horse to drag driftwood to the place he'd picked out for a fence. Once all the usable driftwood was used, he had to dig post holes and plant fence posts cut from tree limbs.

Crawling into his bed that night, he figured it would take two more days to enclose about five acres of flood plain. The wire he'd bought wouldn't turn a thick-hided cow, but it would keep horses inside. That is, if it was kept tight. Which wasn't easy. A wire fence tended to sag in hot weather and snap in the cold. He would have to keep an eye on that fence.

It took three days to plant the fence posts and stretch the wire. He had enough wire for three strands, and he wished he had five. The more the better. The third day it rained, but he kept on working, getting soaking wet, surprised at how cool the rain was. In Texas, the rains were warm and a man didn't mind getting wet. Here, it was cool, and all that kept him from shivering was the hard work. By the time he finished, the rain had stopped, but the sky was still overcast and it held more moisture.

It was good, the rain. In Texas, a good rain was something to celebrate. Rain made the grass grow. With enough rain, he wouldn't have to move the fence until fall.

The next three days he spent horseback. Some of his cattle had ranged as far as twenty miles east of his campsite, and when he found them he found another creek. And more Ladder cattle. This creek was barely a trickle, but cattle could drink out of it, and judging from the tracks, had drunk out of it often.

With whoops and a whirling catch rope, he gathered his cattle, leaving the Ladder cattle behind, and moved them west. He kept them moving until nearly dark, until they could smell water from the better creek, then left them and headed back to his wagon. There, he turned his horse into the pasture, caught another horse and staked that one out. One horse had to be kept handy in case he had to ride for safety, or the other horses pushed the fence down and left the country. He would alternate night horses.

Two days later he had a shelter built. It was nothing but

tarpaper on a rough wooden frame with a blanket for a door. About fifteen by fifteen, with a hole in the roof for a stovepipe. A tin flange surrounded the stovepipe to keep it from burning the tarpaper. Wasn't much, but enough that he could honestly say he'd made some improvements on the land, one of the requirements for gaining ownership of a hundred and sixty acres.

Still, he didn't sleep in the shack, afraid of being trapped inside by scalp-hungry Indians. Instead, he continued to sleep under the trees where he wouldn't be easy to find in the dark.

He would go to town soon, hunt up the land commissioner and file his claim. But first, the rest of his cattle had to be located.

Two days later, riding to his camp at sundown, he saw he had company.

CHAPTER 5

He first saw the men when he rode over a hill, and immediately he turned his horse around and went back to the other side. Dismounting, he crawled on his knees to where he could study them. They were white men. One was in a buggy pulled by two light horses. The buggy had a canopy to shield the man from the sun. Four more were on horseback. Another was on foot, holding his horse by the reins and talking to the man in the buggy.

Mounted again, he rode forward cautiously. They probably weren't dangerous. He'd never known a man in a buggy to be a threat to anyone. But he was ready to wheel his horse around and ride for it just the same.

They saw him coming when he was a quarter mile away, and they stayed still and watched him come. They had Winchesters like his own in saddle boots and they carried six-guns. Two men carried their pistols low on their right hips with the holsters tied down. Professional gunfighters carried guns that way, ready for a fast draw. Bill Williams carried his gun on the left side, butt forward, where it didn't get in the way when he mounted and dismounted and when he rode one horse and led another.

A man who carried his gun low with the holster tied down was ready for a fight. These men were ready for a fight.

No one spoke for a moment when he rode up. He stopped his horse twenty feet from the buggy and waited expectantly. Finally the man on foot spoke:

"How do."

"Evening," Bill said, not moving. "This your wickiup?"

"Yeah," cautiously.

The man who spoke was about forty, average height the same as Bill, but broader in the shoulders. He was one of the two who carried his six-gun low, ready. He had high cheekbones and squinty eyes. Hadn't shaved lately. His flat-heeled boots had no spurs strapped on them, and his hat brim was turned down all around. Looked more like a teamster or a miner than a cattleman. Or a gunfighter.

The man in the buggy spoke then, and for the first time Bill noticed him.

"Chew cand't stay here, chew know."

He was fat, blond, smooth-shaven, with a straw hat, white linen shirt and red suspenders. Sweat ran down his face.

"What?" Bill asked. "What did you say?"

"He said this land is spoke for," answered the man on foot. His voice was neither friendly nor unfriendly.

Bill glanced at the men on horseback. Their faces were expressionless. Three of them looked like cowboys, but the other was dressed like the man on foot and carried his gun the same way.

"Chew vill haf to leaf," said the man in the buggy. "Go. Leaf. Go avay."

Not sure he understood, Bill shook his head. What kind of accent was that? Then he remembered someone in Colorado City mentioning a man named Dutch Aarnstadt, boss of an Eastern conglomerate.

"Are youall with the Ladder?" Bill asked.

"Yeah," said the man on foot. "This land all along here is preempted and most of it's homesteaded. You're camped on our claim."

"Is that right? I don't see any sign of any improvement."

"Doesn't have to be. Not for five years anyway. It's all Ladder territory. The Ladder company's got legal claim to it."

"Chess. Chew vill haf to leaf."

"Reckon you own them longhorns that've been grazin' around here. The ones carryin' an H brand."

"Yeah. They're branded with a Running W too."

The man in the buggy raised his fat hands and let them fall like wounded birds to his lap. "They're a disgrace. Chew haf to get them avay."

Bill didn't know what to say to that so he said nothing.

"Them longhorns are prob'ly carryin' Texas fever," said the man on foot. "Mr. Aarnstadt is afraid the disease will spread."

"They're not diseased," Bill said flatly.

"Chew dond't know. Chew cand't alvays tell."

Still, Bill didn't know what to say, and he looked around at the rest of the men. Finally, another spoke, a skinny galoot with a drooping moustache, a long neck and a prominent adams apple. "Ah'm from Texas too," he said with a drawl, "and Ah know longhorns. Texas fever don't seem to bother 'em, but they c'n give it to Mr. Aarnstadt's good beeves."

"They're a disgrace. They vill haf to go."

"They're not diseased," Bill repeated, "and they've got as much right in this territory as anybody else's stock."

"Huh-uh." The man on foot shook his head. "This is our water. We was here first, and we got a legal claim to it."

Bill shrugged. "You can't claim the whole territory, and even if you've got a legal claim to this water you can't keep anybody else's stock off it unless you fence it."

The man on foot faced him squarely, thumbs hooked inside his gun belt. His face had turned hard, and he squinted up at Bill. "There are ways."

Bill considered that. He was being threatened. He didn't appreciate it, but in a fight he wouldn't have a chance. And, he admitted to himself, he wouldn't want another cattleman moving in on his water. The creek was a long one. There were other places to homestead.

"All right," he said finally, "I'll go to town and see the land commissioner. If you've got a good claim here, I'll move on."

"That's the smart thing to do." The man on foot got on his horse.

"Undt chew must remof those...those awful beasts. They're a disgrace."

Bill had to crack a grin at that. "Those longhorns aren't packing the beef your cattle are, but they'll survive where a better breed won't. Come spring, they'll calve by themselves while you'll lose some, no matter how much riding you do."

"Yeah," agreed the tall thin galoot, "and Lord help any coyote or wolf that picks on a longhorn calf."

"They ain't gonna be here next spring," said one of the men with a tied down holster. "They ain't gonna be here next week."

"Chew must leaf." With that, Dutch Aarnstadt flicked the lines at his team, and the buggy moved forward with a jerk. Two horsemen took the lead, and the rest followed the buggy as the whole outfit moved on.

Bill Williams watched until they crossed a hill and disappeared from sight. Then he rode up to his wagon, dismounted and off-saddled. When he spoke, he spoke to himself. "That was a threat. As clear as anything. What he meant was if I don't move my cattle far away from here, he'll shoot some of them.

"And when men shoot each other's cattle, they end up shooting each other."

His saddle horses needed a rest, so he hitched his Percherons to the light wagon next morning and headed for town. He needed more fence wire anyway, and it was easier to carry in a wagon.

It was a six-hour trip, and just as the town came into sight, he saw four heavily armed men guarding a small herd of horses. He waved. They waved. Then he "Whoaed" his team when he saw one of the men riding at a gallop toward him, obviously wanting to talk.

The man was riding a good horse, part thoroughbred or part hackney, or some other big breed. A good stout horse. Bill Williams held his team still and waited.

"Howdy."

"Howdy."

"Where'd you come from?" He wore a cattleman's boots and spurs and a hat with a high crown and a curled brim. Needed a shave. His voice was friendly.

"About twenty miles east and a little north."

"You homesteadin'?" The horse was fidgeting, stomping its feet, throwing its nose up.

"Yeah. Picked a spot on a creek, on a flood plain."

"Must be Owl Creek. About twenty miles, you say?"

"Yeah."

"Seen any Indians?" He took a sack of tobacco out of a shirt pocket and, holding his reins between two fingers, began rolling a smoke.

Bill shook his head. "Naw. Haven't seen any sign of them."

"They're out there. Killed a couple of kids that was herdin' sheep on Fountain Creek three days ago."

"No." Bill shook his head again, sadly. "Just killed them, huh?"

"Shot 'em and run a spear through 'em and lifted their scalps."

Bill's intestines gathered in a knot as the realization of what he was hearing sunk in. "Has the army been around?"

"Ain't seen hide nor hair of the army. We're gonna have to do somethin' ourselves."

Bill swallowed a hard lump.

"A man alone is a sittin' duck." The horseman struck a match on his saddle horn and lit the cigarette. "If they don't see you you're damned lucky."

All Bill could do was shake his head.

"And if they do see you, they'll kill you and take your scalp too."

"Well, I, uh...I left some horses back there. I've got to go back."

"Better take some men with you and get your horses out of there."

"Yeah, uh, I reckon you're right."

"If you want to join us...we could use another good rifle...if you want to join us, we're gonna do somethin' about these damned murderin' Indians."

"Do you know where they're camped?"

"No, but we'll find 'em."

Bill didn't know what to say. He didn't want war with the Indians. He didn't want war with anybody. Yet, if it came to an all-out war, he wanted to do his part. He couldn't ask someone else to do his fighting for him. "I'll, uh...let me know."

"We'll do it, mister. And," he turned his horse around, "keep your eyes peeled."

Clucking to his team, Bill went on, joining a wagon road where the traveling was easier. Keep his eyes peeled, he did. When he got into Colorado City, he noticed there were fewer people on the streets. He pulled up in front of a livery barn, tied his horses to a hitch rail and went inside, looking for the proprietor. He found him raking manure out of a box stall. The proprietor jumped, startled, and his hand went to the six-gun on his hip when he heard Bill coming.

"Didn't mean to spook you," Bill said. "I'm looking for a place to leave a team of horses for a night."

The stableman relaxed, pulled a blue bandana from a hip pocket and wiped his face.

With his horses unharnessed and locked inside a feed lot with other horses, Bill walked down the street to the land commissioner's office. His boots clomped on the plank walkway, and his spurs rattled. Again, the commissioner's office was locked. Aw hell, Bill said to himself, how the hell can you do business with a man who's never there.

At the stockade, the gate was open, but people and wagons were inside, and two men were keeping watch by peering over the top of the pole wall. There was no room vacant at the Anway Hotel, but he was told the Cascade Hotel down the street had some rooms vacant. He went there.

As he signed the register for a room on the second floor the clerk advised, "Keep your guns handy." He squinted at Bill through small rimless glasses. "The Injuns tried to sneak into town night before last. If they hadn't been seen and shot at they'd of stole everything they could carry."

Indians or no, danger or no, Bill Williams enjoyed the Cascade Hotel. A hot bath in a long tin tub, a shave, clean clothes from the skin out, a good meal in the dining room. He considered a visit to the palaces of pleasure, but first he'd have a shot of whiskey in one of the many saloons.

The first one he came to after he left the hotel was probably as good as any, and he stepped inside. Only four other men stood at the bar, and no one sat at the tables.

"Whiskey," he said to the barman, a husky gent with a handlebar moustache and thick curly hair that grew low on his forehead. A bottle of bourbon was set on the bar in front of him. He poured himself a shot glass full. "Kind of quiet, isn't it?" he said by way of conversation.

"Too damn quite. Damned Cheyennes've got ever'body scared and stayin' home."

"I heard they killed two kids somewhere near here a couple of days ago."

"They did. The sonofabitchin' bloodthirsty heathen bastards. They'll kill anybody with white skin, women, kids, even babies."

Bill took a sip of the whiskey. It burned his throat and stomach and made his eyes water. He blinked his eyes and cleared his throat. "We had...we're having the same kind of trouble in Texas. The damned Comanche hit a ranch, kill everybody they can, steal everything they can, then hightail it out on the Llano Estacado. Nobody has been able to find them out there. Nobody has wanted to find them. There are too damned many Indians."

"The Llano Estacado? I've heard of that. I heard it's a big country, flat as a pancake, where no white man has been."

"Oh, there've been white men out there. Comancheros. They trade with the Comanche. They trade guns for stolen horses and cattle. Whenever a Comanchero is caught, he's hung."

"You've not gettin' any help from the army either, then."

"Not yet. And that's what it's gonna take, an army. A big army." He took another sip of whiskey and felt it settle in his stomach. "I hear it isn't the whole tribe that's causing all the trouble around here, but only a handful of young bucks."

The barman shrugged. "Could be. But it's more'n a handful."

Bill finished his whiskey and tried to decide whether to go to a bordello. He was mulling it over when he heard the yells and the gunshots from outside.

A man yelled, "Over at the barn. They're tryin' to steal the horses." Heavy boots pounded the plank walk. Bill ran outside, a few men from the saloon right behind him. More gunfire. More yells.

Bill ran toward the livery barn, grabbing for the six-gun on his left hip. He had two horses in a feedlot there. He needed those horses. Guns were exploding near the barn. He could see the muzzle flashes in the dark. He ran, hoping the thieves had been discovered soon enough, and hoping he'd get a shot at one of them.

CHAPTER 6

Gunfire was coming from the north end of the barn. Dark shadows moved, and men yelled. "They're out there, to the north. Shoot to the north."

Muzzle flashes came from the dark north of the barn. A bullet whistled past Bill's left ear and *thunked* into the side of the barn. He aimed at a muzzle flash and fired. The .44 boomed and bucked in his hand. He had no way of knowing whether he'd hit anybody. More booms and muzzle flashes. A gun went off so close to his right ear that it started ringing. He fired at another muzzle flash. Now both ears were ringing.

A wild, high, wavering yell came from out there in the dark, and the gunfire and muzzle flashes stopped. Men at the barn continued firing another fifteen seconds, and they too stopped.

Nobody spoke for a moment, then a man asked, "Did they get any horses?"

"Some," a voice answered in the dark. "Old Charlie saw 'em open the gate and he saw some of the horses stampede out, but he got the gate shut before they all got out. Ain't that right, Charlie?" There was no answer.

"Charlie?"

Still no answer.

A scared voice said, "Where's a lantern? Somebody get a lantern."

A lantern was found and lit. Someone carried it into the barn, out again and out to the feedlot gate. "Here he is. He's down."

Men gathered around. The stableman was lying face down in the dirt, his hat beside him and his blood soaking the ground. They turned him over, and the light was held close to his face. His throat and the front of his shirt was a mass of blood.

Someone whispered, almost reverently, "Cut his throat. Damn near cut his head off."

"Yeah. Snuck up behind 'im and cut his throat without lettin' a sound out of him."

"He's dead, ain't he?"

"Has to be." A man knelt over Charlie's body and put an ear to his chest, listened for several long moments, straightened up. His ear was bloody. "He's gone for sure."

A wild curse came from beside Bill. "The goddamn shit-eatin', mother killin' sonsofbitches."

Another joined in the cursing. "Old Charlie never hurt nobody. The bloodthirsty, murderin', God damned heathens."

"Boys, we've stood for this long enough."

"We sure as hell have. Time we hunted up their camp and killed ever' God damned one of 'em."

"Yeah, we've been sayin' that for two weeks now."

"We've been waitin' for the army."

"Waitin', hell. If we wait for the God damned government to do somethin' we're standin' still."

"Standin' still, hell, we're goin' backwards."

"How many horses're left in here."

"Bring another lantern. Let's have a looksee." Someone brought another lantern from the barn. Men crawled through the corral poles. Bill went with them. They walked through the horses, holding the lanterns up.

"Here's a big bay with a blaze face. Who's he belong to?"

"He's mine. One of mine. I had another'n in here, another big bay."

"Here's a big brown horse with collar marks on 'im." A lantern was held up beside one of Bill's harness horses. "Looks like a Percheron. Over here's another'n."

Bill sighed with relief as he scratched the Percheron's neck.

"They're both mine." He shook his head sadly in the dark. "I'm sure obliged to Charlie. I never knew him, but I sure do owe him."

"Yeah. He died tryin' to save our horses."

They walked through the corral, identifying horses. They figured five got out. Someone said, "I'll use mine to help find them five. First thing in the mornin'."

"I'll go too. Them Injuns can't round 'em up in the dark. We'll have to find 'em before the Injuns do."

"You can count on me. I'll be here just before daylight."

"Me too."

More men volunteered. Then someone said, "We got to keep a watch on this pen tonight."

"I'll do it," Bill said.

A light was held up close to his face. "You're a stranger, ain't you?"

"Yeah. But I'll do my part."

"Can we count on you, mister?"

"Come morning I'll still be here," Bill said.

There was more talking, more muttering and cursing, then they all left, two of them carrying Charlie's body. All but Bill. "We're countin' on you, mister."

"I'll stay here," Bill said. And after they were gone, he muttered to himself:

"Dead or alive, I'll be here."

It was a long, dark night. Bill Williams picked the darkest spot he could find near the corral gate and sat on the ground with his six-gun in his hand. He wished he had the night vision and the sharp ears of the Indians. They had the senses of a wolf. No white man could outmaneuver an Indian in the dark. Well, a few white men could. Those few who had lived among them, knew them well, knew all their tricks. Men like Kit Carson.

Was that a horse stamping its feet? Bill's senses were alert, so alert they ached. What was that? A horse blowing its nose, or a savage with a long knife sneaking up on him? Did he pick a good spot? Against the barn would be a better spot. But he couldn't see the gate

37

from there. Had to see the gate. Had to see at least a dim outline of it in the dark. Can't move. Move, and the Indians will know where I am. Stay still. Can't see, so listen. Listen hard.

Ears straining, Bill listened. There was too much noise from the horses. An Indian could sneak up under cover of the horses. His buttocks and his knees ached from staying in one position too long.

What was it some army general once said? The Comanche are the best guerrilla fighters in the world. The Cheyenne and Arapahos are no doubt just as good. Indians have been guerrilla fighters all their lives. They start learning when they're little kids. War is a way of life to an Indian. Before the white man came they fought each other. Always trying to knock each other off their favorite hunting grounds. Every young buck wants to be a war hero.

Don't move.

At first he couldn't believe daylight was coming. The barn was to the east, and when he first saw the outline of the roof against the sky he couldn't believe it. Blinking, he stared hard. Yes, he could see the roof. He looked around, turning his head slowly. Everything else was still dark. His eyes went back to the barn. The roof was a little more visible.

Daylight was coming. They wouldn't try anything now. If they were going to try for the horses again, they wouldn't have waited until daylight. He allowed himself the luxury of straightening his legs. They were numb. He tried wriggling his toes. It worked, and gradually the numbness wore off. He looked at the barn again. It was barely visible, but visible. The corral poles were becoming visible too. He could almost count them. Slowly, he stood, and held himself up by hanging onto a corral post with his left hand. He could see the horses now. And he could see more buildings against the dim light in the eastern sky. He let the hammer down on his six-gun, holstered it and massaged his buttocks with both hands. Then he stretched his legs one at a time. By then he could count the horses. Thirteen.

Sitting again, he waited. When he heard footsteps, his hand went to the gun butt and he drew the gun and cocked the hammer back. As much as he appreciated daylight, he was more vulnerable now. They could see him. The footsteps came closer, coming from around the barn. Men's voices. White men's voices.

He saw them before they saw him. "Over here," he said in a half-whisper.

There were two men. "See you stuck it out," one said. "Spot any more Indians?"

"No."

Two more men joined them. "Let's get saddled. You can bet them Cheyennes are lookin' for them horses."

"Yeah, but I'd like to have more guns. You want to go with us, mister?"

"If you need me," Bill said. "You'll have to loan me a horse. My Percherons are broke to ride, but they're slow."

Four more men showed up, then three more. By good light, a small army was there, some of the men already on horseback. No one offered to lend Bill a horse. The rest got mounted quickly and they all rode out, heading north. Bill watched them go, and when they were out of sight he wondered whether the hotel's restaurant was open yet.

"Damn," he muttered to himself. "I was looking forward to a good night's sleep in a soft bed, and a woman and...aw hell. Damn it all anyway."

At eight o'clock by the big clock on the wall in the hotel lobby, he went out onto the plank walk and turned toward the land commissioner's office. There was traffic on the street, but people talked in hushed tones, as if they feared the Indians would overhear. Walking past a handful of men and women, Bill heard a wrinkled man with a gray beard expounding, "We got to do somethin'. We can't live like this."

Bill had decided that if the land commissioner wasn't there, he'd borrow or rent a saddle horse and try to find him at his home. He just had to get this settled. Did he or did he not have a right to homestead on Owl Creek, on the spot he'd chosen?

He had to know.

At the commissioner's office, he put his hand on the doorknob, expecting the door to be locked again. Well, whatta you know. The knob turned and the door opened.

It wasn't much of an office. Log walls chinked with coarse clay.

Small wood-burning stove with a pipe that went through the wall close to the ceiling. A desk with a wooden swivel chair. And a middle-aged man sitting in the chair with his feet on the desk.

"Are you the land commissioner?" Bill Williams asked.

"I am. James B. Newton is the name." He had a derby hat tilted back on his head and he wore a blue striped shirt with a black bow tie. His thick brown moustache matched the abundance of hair that stuck out from under the hat.

Bill entered the room and stood in front of the desk. "My name is William C. Williams. I'm looking to homestead on a creek about twenty miles east and a little north. I've heard it called Owl Creek."

The land commissioner started shaking his head before Bill stopped talking. "Can't do it. It's taken."

"So I've been told. Can you tell me where on the creek I can homestead?"

The head was still wagging. "Not in this county. You'll have to go almost to Kansas."

"Hmm." Bill studied the wooden floor, then looked back at the land commissioner. "I've been told the Ladder's people have preempted or homesteaded some of the land along that creek, but surely not all of it."

"They have. They've got nineteen quarter sections homesteaded over there, and that gives them about forty-five miles on each side of Owl Creek."

At that piece of news, Bill's eyebrows went up. "Nineteen quarter sections? Forty-five miles? How did they do that?"

"Laid it out an acre deep on each side. Nineteen claims. All they have to do is prove up on it and it's theirs."

"Why that..." Now Bill was shaking his head. "If they claim that much of the creek, they've got control of a hell of a lot of grazing land."

"Indeed they have."

"Nineteen claims?"

"Yes sir."

"There isn't a stick standing along that creek, nor a furrow plowed. Not after you get ten miles out of town. They have to make some kind of improvement."

"They've got five years to do it."

"Uh-huh." Bill studied the floor again, then looked up. "Meantime they've got exclusive use of a big chunk of country."

"You can stake a claim anywhere out there except on Owl Creek."

"Must be half a million acres there that's no good to anybody without water. And the Ladder's got all the water."

"I'd calculate it's at least that much."

"And it's legal?"

"Yes sir."

Shuffling his feet, Bill studied the floor again, then said, "The only way they can claim nineteen quarter sections is to have everybody on the Ladder's payroll file a claim."

"I don't know about that. They filed, just like the Homestead Act says they can."

"Tell me something, Mr. Newton, is there any water in that part of the county other than Owl Creek?"

"I don't know about that. My maps don't show much. The land hasn't been surveyed."

"The way I understand the law, they've got a right to fence off their homesteads, but if they don't fence it off, they have no legal right to complain if somebody else's cattle drink out of the creek."

"Maybe not a legal right, but you can bet they'll do more than complain."

Bill mulled that over. Suddenly he was very tired. The lack of sleep had caught up with him. That and the bad news he was hearing made him feel like he was a hundred years old. He pushed his hat back and rubbed his eyes with the palm of his left hand. He had to make a decision and he didn't feel like making a decision. Turning to go, he said:

"All right, I'll look for more water out that way, and if I find some I'll move. If I don't, well, I don't know what I'll do."

"I hear you've got a fence up."

"Yeah, a few acres for a horse trap."

"You'll have to take it down, you know."

With an angry jerk of his head, Bill said, "Yeah." He left, closing the door behind him.

"Goddamn," he muttered to himself as he walked back to the hotel. "An hour late and a dollar short. Goddamn it to hell anyway."

He went up to his hotel room and gathered his few belongings, then went to the livery barn and harnessed his team. All the time something he couldn't identify kept pulling at his mind. A stop at the mercantile for some groceries was followed by a stop at the hardware store where he bought a few more rods of fence wire and a keg of black gunpowder.

Just outside the town, he flicked the lines at his horses and got them into a trot. Finally, the invisible worry that had been nagging at his mind showed itself.

Someone had told him not long ago that the land commissioner was located only when he wanted to be located. Why was he in his office first thing this morning? He seemed to know everything about Bill Williams and what he wanted. And the subject everybody in town was talking about was the murder of the livery owner, how the Cheyenne had come right into town, cut his throat and run off some horses. James B. Newton had other things on his mind.

Did he just happen to be in his office, or was he expecting Bill? Who told him about Bill? And did somebody also tell him how to answer Bill's questions?

Damn. The land hadn't been surveyed and there was no accurate map. It came to Bill that the Ladder bosses could pick out the land they wanted, do all the paper work for filing a bunch of claims and hire as many men as they needed to sign the papers.

That gave them the legal right to keep everybody else off Owl Creek, and Bill would have to move on.

Dammit, it just wasn't right, it wasn't fair, and maybe it wasn't even legal. But what could he do about it?

All right, he'd move, but not until he found another spot. And, threats or no threats, no damn body was going to hurry him.

He got back to his camp at mid-afternoon, approaching on foot, carrying his Winchester. First, he hitched his team by running the lines under the hub of a front wagon wheel and tying them to a spoke. If the horses tried to move forward, the wheel would turn and tighten the lines, forcing them to stop.

The first thing he noticed was the wire fence was down and his three saddle horses were gone. "Aw, shit," he muttered. Then he saw his tarpaper shack had been knocked down and his cookstove smashed in. His whole camp had been ransacked.

Now he approached with even more caution, his eyes trying to see everything—the camp, the ground, the bluff on the north, the trees, everything. There was no sign of life.

"Goddamn."

Gripping the Winchester with his finger on the trigger and the hammer back, he stood over his pack panniers, saw that everything in them had been dumped onto the ground, saw his saddle was missing, saw flour scattered over the whole mess, turning the ground white in places. He also saw the tracks. Moccasin tracks. Indians.

"Damn it all anyway."

He walked around and saw the horse tracks just outside his camp, on the sandy bottom land. Squatting, he studied the tracks. Four horses. None of them shod. Indians didn't have the steel shoes nor the tools for shoeing horses. Looked like only one man had dismounted and done all the dirty work while the others stayed horseback. Indians, all right.

Bill cussed, but when he thought about the danger he was in he stopped cussing. The Cheyenne knew he had camped here. They knew he was coming back. They would be back.

Realizing that sent an icy chill through his stomach. A hard lump formed in his throat. His hands began to shake and he couldn't stop them. Leave. Get the hell out of here. It's already been claimed anyway.

He'd lost his three saddle horses and his saddle. Next he'd lose his scalp. And his life.

Get out of here, you fool!

CHAPTER 7

Bill Williams walked upstream a way and climbed the bluff. He sat on the ground and studied everything in sight. No Indians now, but they'd be back. For sure, they'd be back. After an attack on a wagon train that gained them nothing and cost them some braves and ammunition, they probably wouldn't attack a bunch of men again, but they'd sure like to catch one or two alone.

Take what's left, load it in that wagon and head for town on a high trot.

Then do what? Leave a hundred and sixty-two head of his cattle to run wild? Wouldn't his brothers hoo-raw him over that. They'd never let him forget it. Well, on second thought, they'd understand. They'd fought the Comanche, and they'd seen the bodies of white men and women murdered by the Indians. No, they wouldn't blame him.

But he'd blame himself.

What to do?

The smart thing to do was to go back to town. There was a lot of talk in Colorado City about how the white men were going to take the war to the Indians. Kick the shit out of them, run them out of the country, and maybe they'd leave the settlers alone. Maybe it would be safe to come back here then.

Yeah, go back to town. That was the smart thing to do.

"But," he shook his head and muttered, "nobody ever said Bill Williams was smart. Goddammit, they've got my horses and I want them." He could ride one of the Percherons bareback and track them down. When he found them he'd...well, he'd at least know where they were. If he found them. "Dammit all anyway."

He went back to the wagon and drove it up to his camp. There, he unhitched the team and stripped the harness off. He staked the horses on the best grass he could find close to camp, and ate a cold supper. A campfire would tell the Indians he was there. Aw shit, he thought, they know anyway.

Gathering wood from under the trees, he laid out enough for a big fire on the sandy bottom land, then he picked up the keg of black powder, pounded the bunghole open, and poured some of the powder around the wood. Next he poured a string of powder on the ground to a spot under the trees, a spot where he unrolled his bed.

With only a little daylight left, he took a sickle he'd bought in Colorado City and cut some grass. He tied the two harness horses to a tree and carried the grass to them. They could eat and they would be close.

Unrolling his bed, he opened it all the way, checking to make sure a rattlesnake hadn't crawled into it. He pulled off his boots, then on second thought he did something he hadn't done in a long time, he unbuckled the spurs, took them off his boots and kept his boots on.

Lying in bed fully dressed, his muscles were tense, his nerves tight. After a while he whispered to himself in the dark:

"Admit it, Bill Williams, you're scared.

"Damned right I am.

"Scared shitless."

About three hours after dark, his nerves suddenly twanged. He jerked upright in his bed. He'd heard something. What was it? The horses?

Ears straining, he listened. Did he hear something or did he imagine it. The cottonwood leaves rustled in the night wind. Was that what he'd heard? Afraid to move, he rolled his eyes upward at the sky. The sky was clear and a half-moon was almost directly overhead.

He rolled his eyeballs back to the wagon, parked in the open on the sandy bottomland. He could see it, barely. Something moved near the wagon. A man. A bareheaded man. Two men. They were moving with caution. Looking for him.

Bill William's heart was beating so fast he was afraid the Indians would hear it as he slowly pushed his bed tarp and blankets down and got out of bed. He gripped the Winchester in his left hand as he fumbled for the matches in his right shirt pocket.

Oh, how he hated to strike a match. As quiet as it was, the sound would carry to the wagon, and the flare of a match would be seen. But there was no other way. First he had to find exactly the right spot. Groping carefully, quietly, he found the rock he'd placed close to his bed. It was something he could strike a match on, and it marked the spot where the trail of black powder ended.

Another Indian had joined the two at the wagon. That made three. There had to be more. Should he wait and see?

Squatting, gripping the rifle in one hand and holding a match in the other, Bill Williams waited. Waited and watched. Listened.

They made no sound. Indians could do that. A whole herd of them could gather at his camp without making a sound. Some people thought they could see in the dark too. Hell, if they could do that they'd see him. No use waiting any longer. He struck the match and put flame to the trail of black pepper. Then he moved fast and got a big tree between him and the wagon.

Hell opened up.

With unbelievable speed, the flame followed the black powder trail to the pile of firewood. It exploded, throwing fire in all directions and lighting up the night.

Bill aimed down the barrel of his Winchester and fired. An Indian fell. He aimed and fired again. Another Indian dropped to the ground.

Return rifle fire came from somewhere. He didn't see where. Four or five shots. A bullet smacked into a tree, but the others didn't come close. The firing stopped.

Now there was nobody for Bill to aim at. The Indians had pulled back into the trees. Bill glanced around. His horses were off to his left. He could see them in the firelight. The Indians would see them and they would be after them.

Bill ran from one tree to another, stopped and watched the

horses. A man's figure appeared beside them. Bill fired. The horses snorted at the gunfire and plunged, trying to break free. The figure disappeared.

Knowing his enemies could see the gunflash, Bill moved fast to another tree. He knelt, wanting to make himself as small as possible. There was no more return fire.

Quiet.

He could hear himself breathing. He tried not to breathe, but his heart was pounding, and he couldn't stop that. Even the horses had quieted. How could the world be so quiet? Listen.

Because every one of his senses was straining, Bill heard—or felt—something behind him. He turned, his finger on the trigger on the rifle. It appeared. Just appeared. A tall dark blob. And it was almost on him.

It knocked his rifle aside, and the shot hit the ground. No chance to lever in another cartridge. It was on him. Bill grabbed the barrel of the rifle in his left hand and held the gun out in front of him like a shield to ward off the attack. The gun stopped the charge of whatever it was, and it grunted. A human grunt.

A knife sliced upward and connected with the barrel. Steel rang on steel. A human hand grabbed the barrel and jerked on it. Bill let go of the rifle, jumped backward and grabbed for the six-gun on his hip. At the same time, in his mind's eye, he could see the body of the livery man at Colorado City with its head nearly severed. A bloody mess. A hell of a way to die. Bill fired point blank at the dark blob, and instantly dropped to the ground.

The blob disappeared. But another appeared. Just above him. A human foot tripped over him, and Bill fired again. A human grunt. Then quiet again.

Bill moved. They knew where he was. There would be more. He moved as quietly as he could, and he moved until he ran into a tree trunk. He went around it, got it between him and the dark blobs, stopped. Listened.

Still quiet. No, something was moving over there.

Squatting again, he kept his feet under him, ready to jump in either direction. His heart was beating like an Indian drum. Something had moved over there, but nothing was moving now. Nothing that he could see.

A fire was still burning near the wagon, still throwing out some light. Two bodies were dimly outlined on the ground. Nothing moved over there either.

The horses were tied to a tree where he'd left them. They were in the firelight. The Indians knew they would be good targets if they tried to steal the horses.

The Indians stayed in the dark. Bill stayed in the dark.

How many were there? Was one sneaking up on him right now?

Thinking about that possibility, Bill's mind again pictured the body of the livery man. His stomach churned with fear.

He waited, crouched, ready, wishing it were daylight and then glad it wasn't. In the daylight they could find him. They had him outnumbered, and they were guerrilla fighters. They would kill him. In the dark he had a chance.

His knees were beginning to ache from squatting. He didn't dare move. Move and they'd hear him. Maybe even see him. Stay still.

Wait.

CHAPTER 8

It was just like the night before. Waiting in the dark, fear keeping him alert. But not keeping his muscles from aching.

Moving slowly, Bill sat on the ground and straightened his knees. He got his back against the tree. Then, on second thought, he lay down. Stretched out on the ground, he was more difficult to see. He lay on his back with his gunhand and gun across his chest. He could see the stars through the treetops, and he watched the stars and listened.

If anything came between him and the stars he would shoot, roll over and shoot again.

Just like the night before. But not quite. Tonight, he'd shot some Indians. How many, he didn't know. But he'd seen two go down near his wagon, and he'd heard two grunt and seen them disappear here in the trees. And tonight he was lying down, his legs straight.

The fire was dying. He could only barely see his horses. Then it was dark everywhere and he couldn't see the horses. The Indians would take them. What could he do about it? Creep over there and guard them? The Indians were watching for him and listening. They had eyes and ears like a wolf. One little move and they'd cut his throat just like they did Charlie's in Colorado City.

But, by God, as long as he was alive they weren't going to take his horses.

Again, moving as slowly and carefully as he knew how, he got to his knees and crawled. Before he put each hand and knee down, he felt of the ground and removed any stick that might break under his weight. It seemed like hours before he could hear and smell the two Percherons. Realizing they were still there brought a small sigh of relief from him. He crawled to the opposite side of the tree they were tied to and lay on the ground.

Daylight came faster this time. First the tree tops were visible, then his horses' heads and ears.

When he could see between the trees he stood. There were no Indians. Had they left in the dark? He couldn't be sure. Carefully, he walked, gripping his six-gun, to the spot where his rifle had been jerked out of his hands and he'd shot two Indians. He found the rifle. And a spot of blood. No Indians.

The birds were back, the meadowlarks, singing their song from tree to tree.

Walking faster now, he went to his bed. From there he could see the wagon and the remains of the fire. Still no Indians. They were gone. They had picked up their dead and wounded and disappeared in the dark.

The morning air was clear and cool, and when he looked at the sky and the horizon, it was hard to believe men had died here just a few hours earlier. But, looking down, there were tracks and spots of blood.

Moccasin tracks. The same kind of tracks they'd left the day before.

Feeling safe for the moment, Bill Williams went back to his horses, untied them from the tree, led them to water, then staked them out on the bottomland grass. He fried some bacon and boiled some coffee and unwrapped the bakery bread he'd bought the day before.

Only a day before? Seemed like a week, what with everything that had happened. Wait 'til his brothers heard about this. He wished the savages had left something behind, something he could show them. A man fights off Indians in the dark by himself, he ought to have something to show for it.

"Huh," Bill snorted aloud. "I've got something to show for it. I've got my scalp. I'll settle for that." Sitting on the sandy ground, he chewed a mouthful of bacon, took a bite of bread and a sip of coffee.

"No, by God, I won't settle for that. They stole my saddle horses. I need those horses. I have to have horses."

The sun was up when Bill Williams caught one of the Percherons and slipped a snaffle bit in its mouth and a work horse bridle with blinders over its head. He noticed with curiosity the tracks left by the Indians' horses. Couldn't tell exactly how many. Six or eight. Must have been a small band of braves trying to steal the rest of a white man's horses and groceries and take a scalp back to their camp to show off to the tribe.

Barefooted horses, same as the day before.

That would make it easier to pick out the tracks of his own horses. They were shod. But another unidentified worry began nagging at Bill's mind. Finally, he shook his head and scrambled up on the big Percheron's bare back. He grinned to himself.

"Good thing you're well fed, old boy. If I have to ride bareback, I'm glad I've got a horse whose backbone is padded with fat. Come on, let's see if we can follow your buddies' tracks."

The tracks were not easy to follow on the grassy prairie. Animals left easier-to-see marks on the desert and in the mountains. Bill had to slide down from the Percheron at times and study the ground between the clumps of wheat grass and yucca. He walked, bent over, studying the ground. At the same time he had to keep looking for hostile Indians.

Doing that, he came face to face with a rattlesnake. It was as long as his arm and almost as big around. Bill jumped back at the same instant the snake struck. It fell short, but immediately coiled again, ready for another strike. The button-like rattles on the end of its tail told Bill it was in a fighting mood.

"Why the hell didn't you rattle before I saw you, you sonofabitch."

After seeing cattle with big painful lumps on their jaws from snakebites, and after watching a good dog die from the venom, he hated rattlesnakes. His hand moved to his six-gun—and paused. A shot could be heard a long way. There wasn't a rock, club or anything else to kill the snake with.

Reluctantly, he stood, went around the snake, far around, and squatted again.

He was parting the grass with his hands when he realized that the shod hoof prints were not among the tracks left by Indian horses. Damn. He straightened up and looked around. What had become of his shod saddle horses? He climbed up on the Percheron again and took another careful look. Did the Indians who stole them take a different route to their camp than the Indians who attacked him last night? They had to be the same bunch of Indians. You'd think they'd head straight back to their camp both times. Unless they were keeping the stolen horses somewhere else. Where in hell could that be?

Now he would have to backtrack and try to pick up the trail of the shod saddle horses.

He went most of the way back to his camp before he cut their sign. They had gone in a different direction, driven by men on barefooted horses. The Indians must be holding them some place. He walked, leading the Percheron, eyes alternating from the ground to the skyline and to every bush and draw where a human could hide. He went on that way for three or four miles, and his stomach was reminding him that he needed food, when he saw something unnatural in one of the brushy draws.

Bill Williams stopped suddenly and dropped to the ground. On second thought he stood. Hell, his horse wasn't about to hide and he might as well be seen too. In fact, he jumped up on the horse, ready to ride for it if necessary. "Huh," he snorted aloud. "Even the scrubbiest of Indian mustangs could catch this big brute. But maybe I can beat them to a ravine or someplace where I've got a fighting chance."

He looked around, trying to locate a spot where he could fort up. There was nothing in sight.

What the hell was that in the brushy draw? Not big enough to be a man, but whatever it was, it was man-made. He touched his spurs to the Percheron's sides and rode on slowly, eyes watching the object. When he got closer, he couldn't believe it. *I couldn't be. Could it?*

Yes, it was. He rode up to it and dismounted, parted the brush and uncovered his stolen saddle. Puzzled, he picked it up and looked it over. Not even damaged. "What in the cotton picking, humped up world...?"

Did they hide it here and plan to come back after it? Or maybe Indians didn't like white men's saddles. Well, anyway, he was mighty glad to have it. Riding bareback was hard on the ass. He pitched the saddle up onto the big Percheron's back. The latigos on both sides had to be let out before he cinched it down. He reached for the stirrup with his left foot, had to jump for it, and got mounted.

Whoever invented saddles and stirrups ought to get a medal, he mused as he rode on, eyes busy.

After another few miles, he was surprised again. Those three horses way over there on the side of a hill, could they be his? When he got closer and recognized the long-legged sorrel, the bay and the dun he used for both a pack horse and a saddle horse. The Percheron recognized them too and nickered in a low gasp.

"Well, by God, you old boys don't know how glad I am to see you."

But what had happened? Did the redskins leave them there and plan to kill Bill, steal his harness team too, come back and throw them all together, then head for their camp?

Yeah, Bill decided, that was the only explanation. Only something went wrong with their plans. Bill wasn't so easy to kill. They had some dead and wounded to take care of.

When he thought about it, Bill was elated. He had his horses back, and the savages were off somewhere licking their wounds. He'd be safe.

For a while. Not for long.

They hated him before simply because he was a white eyes. Now they hated him even more. The brave who could bring back his scalp would be a hero.

Thinking of that, Bill was very tired. He hadn't slept in...how long? Two nights in a row without sleep. Two nights watching for Cheyenne, fearing his throat would be cut any second.

Damn, he thought grimly as he gathered his horses and headed them back to Owl Creek, if they'll just leave me alone for one night, maybe I can catch up on my sleep.

It was late afternoon when he got back. He ran the loose horses into the fenced in pasture, tightened the wire with a pincer tool he used as a wire cutter and wire stretcher, then rode the Percheron in a circle around his camp. He saw no evidence of anyone having been there that day. No new tracks, only old ones. For the second time he studied the tracks left the day before by the Indians who stole his horses. The moccasin prints were exactly like the moccasin prints left by the night marauders. The hoofprints were made by barefooted horses.

Something about those prints didn't jibe, but he couldn't put his finger on it. His mind was turning fuzzy from the lack of sleep, and he couldn't think straight.

"The hell with it," he said aloud.

CHAPTER 9

The night breeze sighed through the cottonwoods, the horses grazed in the cool night air, and the stars looked down on Bill Williams as he slept in his tarp-covered bed. Nothing disturbed him until shortly before daylight. Then he awoke with a snort and lay perfectly still, believing for a second that someone was shining a lantern in his face.

There it was again—a light in his face.

Oh. He grinned at himself sheepishly. It was the half-moon. The breeze was moving the tree limbs and allowing the moon to shine between them. On and off. He went back to sleep. He slept like a dead man.

In the morning, after he'd watered his horses, had breakfast and drank two cups of coffee, Bill Williams felt so good he whistled a tune. This was living. A camp under some cottonwoods, a creek, horses grazing peacefully and good grass as far as a man could see. Almost perfect.

Almost. He stopped whistling.

The savage red men would be after his scalp again. And there was the Ladder. They weren't going to leave him alone.

Well—he resumed whistling—nothing was perfect.

No use rebuilding the tarpaper shack. He'd have to move it anyway. The thing to do that day was get on a horse, a saddle horse this time, and hunt for another place to homestead. There had to be water other than Owl Creek. Let's see. The creek where he'd found some of his cattle had a trickle of water, but he'd be willing to bet it would be dry in another two or three weeks. Unless it rained a lot. Which wasn't likely. But there had to be another stream.

Get horseback, William C. Williams, he said to himself, and find it.

The morning was cool, but soon after the sun came up the air turned hot. Not as hot as Texas, but hot enough to make a man sweat doing nothing. Bill pushed his felt hat back and wiped his sweating forehead with a shirtsleeve. He wished he had a straw hat, the kind Mexicans and farmers wore. He found more of his cattle, but left them alone. They no doubt watered at Owl Creek. Every time he saw trees or what looked like a ravine in the distance he went to it and was disappointed. Lots of streambeds, but no streams. The snowmelt and rain filled some of those hollows in the spring and encouraged trees to grow, but by mid-summer the ground was only damp. He was beginning to think he'd have to go all the way to the Arkansas River to find water, and he knew from traveling through that country, that it wasn't where he wanted to homestead. Almost a desert. Nothing but sand, sagebrush and cane cactus. To the west was the Rocky Mountains. Too damn cold in the winter. And farther south, south of the Arkansas, the country was part of a Spanish land grant, and it could be bought, but not homesteaded. So he'd been told. North was no good either. The pine forest was as cold as the mountains.

That left only the east. Bill turned east.

When the sun was straight up, he stopped, loosened the cinches on his double-rigged Texas saddle, hobbled his horse and ate a lunch of dried beef and bread. Being a cattleman he never carried a canteen. Where there were cattle there was water not too far away. Come to think of it, he hadn't seen any cattle for the past two hours.

Mounted again, the turned northeast. "I'm spitting cotton," he said to the horse. "We've got to find water or we'll dry up and blow away."

By mid-afternoon he came to Owl Creek again, but east of his camp. He guessed he was fifteen miles east of his camp, but he had no way of knowing whether he was still in Ladder country. Probably was. His horse drank out of the creek. Bill lay on his belly and drank too.

All right, he said to himself, standing, we'll go on and just see where this creek goes. Who knows, it might join another creek somewhere. He mounted, then reined up sharply, eyes squinting at the eastern horizon.

Riders were coming. A lot of riders.

They hadn't seen him, and they weren't coming his way. Instead they were traveling west and were a little south of him. And he could tell from the way they sat their horses and how the horses moved that they were tired. Bone weary. A wagon pulled by a two horse-team followed the riders, bouncing over the grass. They were white men.

Bill touched spurs to the dun gelding and rode toward them at a gallop. They saw him coming then and stopped. When he got closer, one rider split from the bunch and came toward him. Bill recognized the man.

"Joel Hoskins," Bill said when they met. "Youall look like an army that more than met its match."

"No," Hoskins shook his head sadly, "we whupped 'em. Killed eighteen Injuns."

"What?" Bill was astonished. "Killed Indians?"

"Yeah. Forty-nine men livin' in and around Colorado City got together and asked me to help 'em find the Cheyennes' camp. I useta live with the Cheyennes. I knew where they might be."

"You did?" All Bill could do was stare, first at Joel Hoskins and then at the riders. They were a ragtag bunch, riding all kinds of horses and wearing all kinds of clothes, from bib overalls to baggy wool pants. Their weapons ranged from long muzzle loaders to short carbines.

Hoskins pulled a tobacco sack from a shirt pocket and rolled a smoke. "I didn't much want to do it 'til I seen them two kids that was scalped south of Colorado City." He turned in his saddle and yelled at the men. "Go on. I'll catch up." His faded eyes were sad. He still wore the buckskin shirt and still had his hair in a long braid that hung down his back.

"Well hell," Bill said. "It had to be done. They came after me a couple of nights ago. I fought them off in the dark."

He studied Bill's face. "Hell you did. How'd you do that?"

"I was ready for them. They made a mistake coming in the dark. If they'd come in the daylight I wouldn't have lasted ten minutes."

"Wal, they won't give you any more trouble. Only a few of the bucks got away. We tried not to hit any squaws or kids and let them go. They took some of their dead, and we buried the rest. We found some scalps hanging in their teepees."

"Where did they go?"

"South. I don't know where they'll end up. They'll behave. You can bet on that."

"How far away were they camped?"

"Just over that hill yonder."

Bill shook his head in wonderment. "You must have caught them with their britches down."

"That we did. We waited until first light and run their horses off and then opened fire."

"Any white men killed?"

"Two dead and two hurt. Both the dead men had wives. I hate to go back with 'em and see their wives."

"Yeah." Bill looked down. "Damn it to hell anyway. Always somebody killing somebody."

"That's a fact."

Both men were silent a moment, each with his own thoughts. Then Hoskins said, "Wal, I got to go. We won the battle, but we're a beat up bunch. It's a long way to town."

"Well, tell the men that I and folks like me owe them a debt. I'm surely obliged."

Hoskins turned his horse around. "I'll tell 'em that."

Bill watched them go. Sat his horse and watched them for a full fifteen minutes. "Damn," he said to himself, "what a goddamn cruel world."

At first he thought he'd go back to his camp. Then he realized he hadn't accomplished what he'd set out to do that day. And when he thought about it, he realized also that the Indian camp had to be on a creek. Far enough away from town that the Ladder wouldn't have the creek preempted.

Curious, he turned his horse east again. The Indian camp, what was left of it, was supposed to be just over that hill. A column of smoke rose a hundred feet over there and then was dissipated by the westerly breeze. No telling what he'd find.

At the top of the hill he could see the fires. Looked like everything had been tossed into one big pile and two smaller ones and set afire. The two smaller heaps of ashes and the charred remains of something man-made had almost burned themselves out and were barely smoldering.

Bill sat his horse and shook his head sadly. If he'd known, if they'd asked, he would have joined the battle. But as he stared at the ruins he was grateful that he hadn't had to. Defending himself was one thing, attacking and killing Indians was something else. He couldn't blame the settlers for doing it, but he was glad he hadn't taken part in it.

There was a creek. Owl Creek joined another creek here and they both meandered southeast, probably to the Arkansas. Where they passed by the Indian camp, the brush, chokeberry bushes or something, grew dense, covering a good two acres. A half-dozen cottonwood trees were scattered along the far bank.

He rode into the ruins. Nothing stood. The wigwams had been torn down and either carried away by the squaws or burned. A few white men's cooking utensils remained. Pots and a big black iron kettle. Stolen, no doubt. The kettle would come in handy, but he couldn't carry it horseback. Wooden handles had been burned off the pots and tin pans. Without dismounting, he prowled through the ruins, wishing he could have seen how the Indians lived before the attack. What they ate. What they made their shelters out of. What they slept on, now that buffalo robes were scarce. Did they have blankets plundered from wagon trains and settlers' cabins? Probably. Or maybe the government gave them blankets.

Not a living creature was in sight.

Bill felt a shiver run up his back. Only a short time earlier a fierce battle had taken place here. Men had died. Now there was nothing.

Ghostly.

He rode to the creek and found a path that led from the camp to a spot where the water was clear and deep. A well-used path. A good place to camp, to homestead. Had to be far enough away from Colorado City that the Ladder had no claim to it. Bill allowed his horse to drink from the creek, then rode back to the ruins. Yep, a good spot. Easy to identify on a map. Only a day's travel in a wagon to Colorado City and a day's travel back. Ideal.

Except for the ghosts.

It occurred to him that the dead had to be buried nearby. Joel Hoskins had said the squaws carried some away and the rest were buried. Bill rode in a half circle around the camp, looking at the ground, then crossed the creek and rode to the top of a grassy hill. There he found the graves. Eight, with fresh dirt and rocks piled on them. Might have been more than one body in each grave.

It was quiet. Even the birds were quiet. Eerie.

Someday somebody would homestead here. A cabin would be built near the bushes and the creek. Grass would grow over the graves, and somebody's stock would graze on them. The story of the battle would be told and retold a thousand times.

But could Bill Williams live here? He shook his head sadly. It was something to think about.

He rode back to the creek, then out of curiosity, to see where the second creek came from, he rode upstream, keeping in the water. In places the water was over his horse's knees, but the brush was so thick a horse couldn't travel on the bank, and he had to stay in the water. If he homesteaded here, he'd have to cut away some of that brush. Or maybe the longhorn cattle would make some trails through it. Cattle were good trailmakers. He saw that the second stream came from the north, almost straight north. It was a small stream, but the two together created a creek that wouldn't run dry. Not even in the driest years.

Yep, a good spot.

But there was that shiver up his spine again. He felt as though the dead were watching him, resenting him. He felt as though he had no business here. He was in Owl Creek now where the water was only halfway up to his horse's knees. He held the animal still, looking and listening to the quiet. Suddenly his back stiffened and his senses came alert. Taut. A noise. Like a small animal. An animal in a trap.

He kept his horse still and listened. There it was again. Back in the brush. A rabbit in a trap? Indians knew how to trap the cottontail rabbits and probably considered them good food. Yeah, that's what it was. Had to be.

No use letting the little brute stay there and die. Might as well set it free. If he could find it. He rode out of the creek and into the brush, stopping every few yards to look. The brush was so thick he had to duck his head and let the hat protect his face. If an old cow got in here and didn't want to be caught, she wouldn't be caught. Bill reined up again and looked at the ground around him, what he could see of it. He rode on a few yards and stopped again. What he saw there made him suck in his breath.

He couldn't believe it.

CHAPTER 10

She had straight black hair that framed her face. Black fearful eyes that stared at him. She lay on her back with her knees drawn up and her legs apart. Her buckskin dress was pulled up around her waist. She tried to move, got up on her elbows, then fell back.

"Good Godamighty," Bill muttered. "She's having a baby."

He dismounted quickly and went to her. She tried to shrink within her body, away from him. "Don't worry, little squaw," he said, trying to talk in a soothing voice. "I won't hurt you."

Kneeling, he could see the top of the baby's head, barely showing. It had wet, sparse, black hair.

"You picked a fine time to calve," he said, still trying to talk in a calm, quiet manner. "Looks like you need some help."

The black eyes continued staring at him. She was young. Hard to tell how old. Around twenty. Maybe younger. Can't tell about a squaw.

"This your first one?" He knew she couldn't understand. "Heifers calving for the first time sometimes need help. Let's see now..."

He'd pulled many calves into the world and even a few colts. But a human baby? He hadn't even seen a human baby born.

She grunted and strained. The baby's head came a little farther, then was sucked back in.

"Something ain't right," Bill muttered. "Ain't coming out right."

He rocked back on his heels and tried to figure out what to do. Let's see. A calf comes out with its forefeet right beside its nose. Sometimes a foreleg gets doubled back, and a man has to reach in and straighten the leg. How about a human baby? How was it supposed to come out?

She strained again. Gritted her teeth and strained. Nothing happened.

"Well, I hate to do this," Bill said. "This is gonna hurt. But if I don't do it you'll both die."

He rolled up his shirt sleeves, knelt between her legs and poked two fingers into her vagina beside the baby's head. Watching her face, he got one hand in and groped for the baby's shoulder.

"Uh-oh. Here's the trouble." One of the baby's arms was out of place. Across the chest. Not straight the way he guessed it was supposed to be.

She groaned and gritted her teeth as he pushed his hand in farther and tried to straighten the baby's arm. "I know it hurts. I never had a baby and never will, but I know it hurts." His right hand was in up to his wrist and he was afraid the vagina would tear, but he had to do what he was doing. Trying to do.

She had the back of her hand over her mouth, holding back a scream, as he pushed the baby's arm down to its side, straightened the hand. He realized he was sweating with tension, and he wiped sweat off his forehead with the sleeve on his left arm. Slowly, he withdrew his right hand. It was wet with slime. "All right, young lady, try again. Give it a good try."

She tried. The baby's head moved. It was coming out. Should he take hold and pull? That's what he would have done if it were a calf. He'd pulled on calves with his hands and with a rope, and he'd even used horse power to pull calves out. She strained again. The baby didn't move.

"All right. I'll try to help." He got his fingers under the baby's chin and pulled gently. It moved. Soon he could get his fingers under its armpits. He pulled gently again.

And then the baby was born. A slimy little creature, with a brown body, black hair and a pinched face.

Bill rocked back on his heels and breathed a sigh of relief. "A bull calf," he said. "You've got a brand new son." He was proud of himself. Midwife to a squaw. Hell, to a woman. Red or white, she was human. Then he realized the baby wasn't breathing.

"Uh-oh. Now what?"

A cow would lick the baby's face, clean the slime off its mouth and nose and it would start breathing. He wasn't a cow, but he had learned from cows. He untied the black silk bandana from around his neck and carefully wiped the baby's nose and mouth. "There. That ought to do it."

The umbilical cord was still intact, from the vagina to the baby's navel.

"Come on little man, breathe." It still wasn't breathing. Now what?

"All right, if I gotta I gotta." He laid the baby by its mother's side, on its back, then knelt over it. "There's things I'd rather do," he muttered, as he placed his mouth over the baby's mouth.

With one hand on the baby's chest, he blew into its mouth. The chest swelled. He sucked, then blew again. Straightened up. Looked at the mother's face. She was watching him with her black eyes. He knelt, blew into the baby's mouth, sucked.

Suddenly, the baby gasped, inhaled and let out a small cry.

"Atta boy. Come on, you can do better than that."

Another cry, and then a squall.

"Atta boy." Bill's face split into a wide smile. He looked at the mother's face. She wore no expression. "Hey, little gal, you've got a baby boy. Just listen to that little feller holler."

She tried to sit up, fell back, weakly. She tried again. Couldn't. One brown arm moved and reached down for the baby.

"Good idea," Bill said, happy with what he'd accomplished. "This little man needs to suck now." Her leather dress had no buttons, only a split down the front. She tried to pull the top down off her shoulders, fumbled with it. "Here, let me help."

Bill put his hands on her shoulders and pulled the dress down.

"Oh my God." He hadn't really realized what he was doing until the breasts were exposed. Small round breasts. Full. Brown nipples. A woman's breasts.

For a moment, he stared. He'd almost forgotten how beautiful a woman's breasts could be. Under his breath, he murmured, "Oh my God." All he could do was stare until finally the baby's squalling brought his mind back to where it belonged. "Oh, uh, excuse me." He got his hand under the baby and laid it beside her right breast. The umbilical cord wouldn't reach much farther.

A cow would chew the cord in two, he knew, but how about a human mother? The baby was nursing. It knew what to do. But Bill didn't know what to do about that umbilical cord. Cut it off? Maybe. Maybe not. Did she know what to do? Yeah, she ought to know what to do.

He reached into his chaps pocket for the folding knife he always carried, opened the biggest blade and put it beside her right hand.

"Don't know if this is the kind of tool you need," he said, "but it's the only tool I've got."

She was watching the baby, then she quietly watched him.

"Go ahead." When she didn't move, he said, "Oh, sure. All right."

He stood and turned his back to her, and when he did that he realized he had another problem. What to do about her. She couldn't walk and probably wouldn't be able to walk for some time. She'd just had a rough calving. A very rough one. She was a sick young woman. He couldn't put her on a horse and he couldn't just leave her here. He thought it over and turned back to her. She hadn't moved.

"Here's what I'm gonna do, young lady. I'm gonna go to my camp and get my team and wagon, and then I'm gonna come back for you. Understand?"

The black eyes watched him without blinking.

"You don't understand. Wish I could make you understand. Here." He took off his shirt and wrapped it around the baby. "It'll be dark when I get back. Don't move. If you do I'll have a hard time finding you in the dark." He stood before her, bare-chested, missing his shirt already.

"I'll be back. Don't move."

Bill Williams went to his horse, gathered the reins and stepped into the saddle. The woman watched him with round black eyes. He rode through the brush, his bare chest and shoulders collecting a dozen scratches.

Once out of the brush, he stopped and looked back for a landmark of some kind. The smallest cottonwood on the north, and, uh, the biggest pile of ruins on the south. She's right between the two, not far from the creek. Hope that moon comes out and I hope it's a bright one.

A three-quarter moon was straight overhead, and Bill guessed it was a couple of hours before midnight when he got back to the ruins. He'd kept his team going at a steady trot, the wagon bouncing over the rough ground. The horses were glad to stop when they got to the thick bushes that grew along the creeks.

He hitched the team to a wheel hub and lit the lantern he'd brought. The trees were easy to see, but the fires were completely burned out, and Bill had to hunt for the biggest pile of ruins. When he found it he stood between it and the cottonwoods on the far bank. He picked out the smallest of the trees, took four steps to his left and believed he was directly between that tree and the charred mess behind him. She should be straight ahead. Now he had to push his way through the bushes. He was glad he owned more than one shirt.

Holding the lantern and bending low, he pushed branches aside with his left hand, held his head down to let his hat brim take most of the punishment, and stumbled on into the bushes. He stumbled over something, held his lantern down and saw it was a root. Stopping now and then to get his bearings, he went on.

The next thing he saw was water. He was out of the brush and on the edge of the creek. He'd lost his bearings. Or she'd moved.

"Damn," he muttered. "Hard enough to find anything in here in the daylight. All right, where's that damned tree." He looked across the creek at the trees. "Aw dammit. They looked different from here. Can't tell which is the littlest."

He called for her, "Hey. Hey little squaw, it's me. I came back for you." He listened. No answer. "Hey, where the hell are you?"

He pushed his way into the brush again. Stopped every few yards and held his lantern close to the ground. "Dammit," he muttered again, "am I gonna have to camp here and wait for daylight? No sir. Not with those graves over there. Those Indians hated white eyes so much, one of them might raise up out of his grave and slit my throat. Come on, little woman."

He saw horse tracks. Now he knew where he was. Turn a little to the left. He held the lantern close to the ground and found her,

She hadn't moved. He put the lantern close to her face. She stared at him without expression. The baby was still wrapped in his shirt. Its eyes were closed and it appeared to be asleep, cradled in her left arm. In the lantern light he saw that she had cut the umbilical cord and had pulled her dress down.

"Why didn't you answer me? Scared, huh? Don't blame you. Well, we've got to get you away from here. To my camp. Don't know where else to take you. Folks in town don't care whether you live or die. Come on."

His folding knife was on the ground beside her. He picked it up, closed the blade and put it in his chaps pocket. Then he placed the baby on her chest, got his left hand under her shoulders and his right hand under her knees. He straightened up, lifting her off the ground. With two fingers of his right hand, he got hold of the lantern bail.

The brush was so thick that at times he had to turn around and walk backward, pushing his way. She was light. Just a little bit of a thing. The baby stayed quiet.

At the wagon, he put her on his bed in the back and put the pillow under her head. Still, she made no sound, only watched him with those round black eyes. He gathered the lines and climbed to the seat. Turning to look back at her, he said, "I'll take it slow. Won't bounce you around any more than I have to."

He blew out the lantern and clucked to the team. As the wagon moved ahead he thought about it and worried about it and he couldn't think of an answer to the question that wouldn't leave his mind:

What the humped up hell was he going to do with her?

CHAPTER 11

Every time a wagon wheel bounced, he winced. Not because he felt any pain but because he believed she did, though no sound came from her. About halfway to his camp the baby woke up and started crying. Wailing.

Bill Williams had seen very few human babies and knew nothing about them. He "Whoaed" the team and lit the lantern. Just as he did that the baby stopped crying. By the light of the lantern he saw that it was nursing. He grinned.

"Hungry little booger, ain't you. Just like a sucking calf, knows where dinner is."

The woman kept her mouth shut and looked at him without expression.

Rather than follow the meandering creek, he tried to take a direct route to his camp, but there were no landmarks, and at first light he realized he'd gone about a quarter mile too far. By the time he got to his camp, it was broad daylight.

First he lifted her out of the wagon, laid her on the ground and took his bed and spread it out near the pushed-over tarpaper shack. Then he carried her over to the bed. She tried to stand, but immediately collapsed. He got her in the bed and covered her up.

"You probably ought to have a doctor," he said, "but I don't think you could stand a wagon ride that far. And I don't know how a white-eyes doctor would treat you anyway. Folks in this territory ain't too fond of Indians."

After stripping the harness off the team, he watered all his horses, checked his fence, then set about cooking breakfast. The young squaw had her eyes closed and appeared to be sleeping. The baby was also sleeping. He fried some bacon and made a pot of coffee. A full stomach made him drowsy, but he didn't want to sleep. He had some riding to do. Had to locate the rest of his cattle and find another place to camp. Couldn't afford to sleep in the daylight.

At the creek, he splashed cold water on his face, filled a canteen and went back to the wagon. She was awake, watching him. "How about some breakfast, little squaw?"

No answer.

"Got to eat. Can't get well if you don't eat."

Still no answer. "Well, how about a drink of water?" He went to her, put an arm under her shoulders, lifted her half up, and handed her the canteen. She took it in both hands and drank, first a tentative swallow, then four more. Her black hair hung straight down below her shoulders, and he could see where it had been cut off to keep it from growing all the way to the ground.

"All right, now how about something to eat? What do Indians eat for breakfast? Bacon? Flapjacks? Naw, you probably don't know what that is. Well, you can try."

He put more wood on the fire and fried two thick strips of bacon. He lifted her head and shoulders again and handed her a strip. "Careful, it's hot. I'd give it to you on a plate, but maybe you wouldn't know what to do with a knife and fork."

Her hand touched his briefly as she took the strip of bacon. It was a small feminine hand. Brown, but feminine. She put the bacon to her lips and took a small bite. While she chewed, he cut a thick slice of bread and handed that to her. She chewed slowly, and when she had all the bacon and half the bread down, she suddenly fell back. Her eyes closed and stayed closed for a moment, then opened, watching him.

"Pretty weak, huh? Maybe what I ought to do is cook you something that's easier to chew. What would that be? Oh, I know."

It took time, time he didn't want to spend in camp, but he opened a sack of rolled oats and dropped a double handful in a small iron pot of boiling water. "It won't stick to your ribs like sowbelly, but it's good for you. That's what they say, anyhow." He realized he was talking to himself as much as to her. And that made him realize it was lonely, camping by himself. He wished she could talk to him. When the oats were a soft gummy mess, he ladled some into a tin bowl, added a few drops of canned, condensed milk, and took it to her.

Again, he had to lift her up and hold her. She took the bowl but made no move to eat. "Oh, excuse me, you need a spoon, don't you." She held herself up with her hands under and behind her while he found a spoon and brought it back to her. Still, she made no move to eat.

"Like this, see." He took the spoon, dipped it full of boiled oats and lifted it to his mouth. "See?" He handed it to her and held her up with one arm under her shoulders. She got the idea and, with a shaking hand, took a spoonful. Her face was expressionless as she tasted it.

"Tastes Godawful, I know, but it's good chuck. It'll help you get your strength back. Maybe a little sugar would help."

But she didn't need the sugar. She ate a dozen spoonfuls, and put the bowl down almost empty. "Well," he said, as he let her lie back, "at least you got something into you. That little feller's got his breakfast all ready for him anytime he wants it." Before he rode out of camp that morning, he took another look at her. She was lying on her back with her head on his pillow. Her eyes were open and she was staring at the sky.

She looks comfortable, he thought. But when I get back where in hell am I gonna sleep?

Bill Williams was a very tired man when he rode in that evening. Tired and discouraged. He had located most, if not all, of his cattle, but at least half of them were watering on the small creek that was drying up fast. Without a heavy rain it wouldn't last much longer. He had gone beyond that creek, looking for another. Every tree, every bushy gulch had to be checked, and by mid-afternoon he was beginning to understand why the conglomerate had claimed all of Owl Creek. There didn't appear to be any other dependable source of water. Turning back, he had gathered his cattle into a big bunch and driven them north. When he was convinced that they knew where Owl Creek was he let them go. "Go and propagate," he said with a wry grin. "That's what the cow business is all about."

And all day he worried about her. Would she be there when he got back? Maybe, just maybe, some of her people would come along and claim her. Maybe, but not likely. Her people, what was left of them, probably thought she was dead. And unless she had remarkable recuperative powers, she was too weak to leave on her own. He wondered where her people went. He wondered if she knew where they went.

The last thing he needed was a sick woman and a baby. But— he grinned when he thought about it—that little black-haired kid was as cute as a newborn puppy.

She was still there, but she had moved. Somehow she had gotten out of the bed and moved the bed under a cottonwood, in the shade. She was lying on top of the bed tarp when he rode up.

Of course. He should have known. Everybody, sick or well, has to relieve himself. Or herself. Exactly how she had managed that when she was too weak to walk, he didn't know. Crawled, maybe? Crawled and dragged the bed?

She was awake, staring at him again when he rode up. "Evening Little Mouse," he said pleasantly. Without dismounting, he looked around the camp, at the marks on the ground. "Yep," he said to himself, she crawled.

Bill Williams didn't consider himself an expert tracker, but he had located a lot of cattle on the vast plains of Texas by following tracks. And he could see that she had walked on her hands and knees.

Every time he looked at her he found her looking at him. No expression on her face at all. The baby was lying beside her, wrapped in his shirt, asleep. He dismounted, off-saddled and watered his horse. Then he built a fire and put a dutch oven half full of water over the fire. That done, he watered the rest of his horses and turned them all loose in his small pasture.

He'd bought a shoulder of beef the last time he was in town and hung it, wrapped in canvas, in the shade of the trees. Now he cut off two small steaks, went back to his fire and peeled three potatoes. His supper was a tough steak, boiled potatoes and gravy made of flour and water. But first he fed her. She took the meat in her hands and ate slowly. Tough as it was, she seemed to have no trouble chewing it. She had good strong white teeth, he noticed.

"Glad to see you eating," he said. "Have some spuds." He handed her a plate of potatoes and gravy and a fork. She took it, watched him eat, stabbed a potato with the fork and tried to emulate him. She was awkward, but she cleaned the plate.

Bill grinned. "I do believe you're gonna live, Little Mouse." He realized then that he had named her. Well hell, got to call her something, and she ain't much bigger than a mouse. Just a little bit of a thing. Pretty sick last night and this morning, but looking better now. Looks more alive. Wonder how old she is. Somewhere between sixteen and twenty, I'd guess.

He took the plates, knives and forks to the creek, scraped them bare with sand and washed them. Out of the corner of his eye he saw her get up, first on her knees, then on her feet. She stood for about ten seconds, then dropped onto her knees again. When she saw him watching, she tried again to stand, but got only halfway up before she collapsed. Her leather dress had once been a beautiful tan color, but was turning dark now in the worn places. Bill had seen and handled buckskin before, but he'd noticed when he'd carried her that her dress was made of the softest leather he had ever handled. Nobody can tan leather like an Indian, he'd heard. The commercial tanneries couldn't even come close.

Just before dark she tried again to stand, got to her feet, but dropped onto her knees again. She left the baby on the bed and crawled on her hands and knees. Bill started to help her but realized she needed privacy.

While she was gone he took one of the blankets from his bed and prepared to spend the night wrapped in one blanket under the wagon. And when he saw her coming back, crawling, he went to her and helped her to her feet. With his help, she took a half-dozen steps before her knees buckled. He carried her the rest of the way.

"Wish I could get you to a doctor," he said, shaking his head sadly.

She lay back, gathered her baby to her and closed her eyes.

* * *

It was an uncomfortable night for Bill Williams. One blanket didn't make a comfortable bed. In the morning, he would rebuild the tarpaper shack. Though he didn't expect to leave it there long, they needed a shelter of some kind until the squaw got well enough to travel. At breakfast she ate bacon, tried the coffee, put the cup down, and finished the slice of bread. While Bill worked on the shack, she crawled away downstream again.

When he finished he was surprised to see her standing. Her face was still blank, but she took a determined step, then another. Four steps later, she sat on the sand. The baby started crying, and she crawled back to him.

He wished she would speak. Say anything. He wouldn't understand, of course, but it would be nice if she would at least try to communicate. He was tired of talking to himself. But then it really made no difference. As soon as she was strong enough, she'd leave. He'd come back to his camp one day and find her gone. Well, that's the way it should be. Had to be.

Riding the bay pack horse, Bill went back to the scene of the battle, and, trying to ignore the ruins, followed the two creeks from their junction, hoping they would curve back west. After about ten miles of riding east, he saw they turned south, and after another five miles found himself on a desert with nothing but yucca, sand and cane cactus. Not good cattle country. If that wasn't discouraging enough, the creek, whatever it was called at that point, was petering out. Seepage and evaporation had reduced it to a foot-wide trickle. Bill reckoned it couldn't be depended on the year around every year.

That did it. He'd have to gather his cattle and move them to another territory. Where, he didn't know. He'd have to do a lot of exploring. But first, he had to get that squaw well and on her way. Out of his way.

Come to think of it—Bill reined up and sat his saddle deep in thought when the idea struck him—that squaw might know of a good spot. Her people had lived on these plains for a lot of years. They knew every creek, spring, rock, bluff and tree. She was young, but she'd moved around. Those Indians could have their camp packed and ready to move in a couple of hours. Or less. They were always moving. That is until the government tried to tell them where they could live and where they couldn't.

No wonder they hated white-eyes.

Well, that wasn't his doing. He had to live too. And even if she wanted to help, he couldn't tell her what his problem was, and she couldn't tell him anything either.

She had a fire going when he rode up and dismounted. She was sitting by the fire, and had a pot of something in the middle of it. She stood when she saw him coming, but sat again.

"Evening," Bill said. She said nothing. Her black hair was parted in the middle and hung halfway down her back.

Whatever was cooking smelled good.

His three saddle horses were looking a little gaunt, and Bill knew he was going to have to move the fence to fresh grass. He needed a couple more horses too. When a man rode all the time, three grass-fed horses weren't enough. In Texas, a cowman needed eight or ten to stay horseback.

Problems were mounting. What he ought to do, he thought, was gather his cattle, drive them to Cheyenne, sell them and go back to Texas. He'd have to have help. Gathering and moving that many cattle was too much for one man. Well, if that was what he decided to do he could hire someone in Colorado City.

But that wasn't what he wanted to do. He wanted to stay here. As a cattleman, he believed the first to use the land, to settle on it, ought to own it, and he had no quarrel with the conglomerate. He only wished he could find water and a place to homestead somewhere between the desert to the south and the cold pine forest to the north, but so far he'd had no luck. And he wanted to do everything legally, the right way. Yeah, he had problems.

She studied his face when he walked back to the fire, and then her face changed expressions too. It was the first time he'd seen any expression at all on her face. A worry wrinkle appeared between her eyes, and she looked at him with—what? Understanding? Naw. Couldn't be. Yet that was definitely a worry frown, and those big black eyes had softened. Her face, Bill noticed for the first time, was oval, with high cheek bones, a straight nose, and straight mouth and chin. Dark complexion, but, yeah, when you look at her, kind of pretty. Like a Mexican girl. There was no girl prettier than a pretty Mexican girl, and maybe Indian girls were the same.

What she had cooking was a stew. Bill looked over at the canvas-wrapped hunk of beef shoulder hanging from a tree limb, and saw that she had unwrapped and rewrapped it. There were potatoes and carrots in the stew, and just enough water to make a thick gravy. Marks on the ground told him that she had walked a way, sat a while, and walked a way. She had also crawled in places.

The stew needed salt, but with that added it was delicious. Sitting cross-legged on the ground, Bill ate so much he thought he would pop. He grinned, patted his stomach and said, "Good." He said it again, grinning, "Good." She had eaten a plateful herself, using a fork to eat the chunks of potato and carrot, and using her fingers to eat the meat. Bill grinned and said it a third time, "Good."

Her face twitched. Just a small twitch. "Good," Bill repeated, and grinned broadly. Another twitch, then a quick smile. It disappeared immediately.

"That's the way. Smile. It doesn't hurt."

Suddenly, she busied herself, stood and gathered the dirty plates, knives and forks. Moving awkwardly, she started toward the creek, fell onto her knees, stayed there a minute, and stood again. Bill went to her and tried to help, but she shook her head negatively and uttered the first sound he had heard from her. It was nothing but a grunt, but he got the message: she didn't want any help. She wanted to do it alone.

That night his one-blanket bed wasn't so hard. Was it because he was too weary to care? Anyway, he slept fairly well.

Next day he found himself in a horse race.

CHAPTER 12

He was riding his long-legged half-thoroughbred sorrel, following the creek east, wondering how far he'd have to go to get out of Ladder territory and away from the Indian ghosts. He grinned to himself when he thought about it. So I'm superstitious. I believe in ghosts. Well, not really. Well maybe. Aw hell, who knows. If he went far enough east he'd be out of anyone's territory, and he could carve out some territory of his own. He'd hoped he wouldn't have to be more than a day's drive in a wagon from a settlement. A man needed supplies and building materials and grain for the horses in the winter. But if he had to pick a spot more than a day's drive away, he would.

It was about noon when he saw the horses. A half-dozen of them, just about every color and size. Long manes and tails. Wild. No, he saw when he got closer, not wild.

They saw him at the same time he saw them, and they made no move to run. Instead, they stood with their heads up watching him come.

Indian horses. Had to be. The settlers ran the Indians' horses off before they opened fire on the camp. Without horses, the Indians couldn't get away. The rest of their horses were probably scattered over eastern Colorado Territory by now. Bill rode closer, looking them over. They moved away.

Just like the remuda horses on the Running W down home. Once a man got his hands on them they were gentle enough, but catching them wasn't always easy.

Bill could use more horses. Hell, he needed more horses. Did these belong to anyone who could catch them? He didn't know. At least four of them were mustangs, wild horses the Indians had caught and broken to ride, but two had some breeding in them. Stolen. They belonged to some settler somewhere. If he didn't catch them right now, whoever they belonged to would probably never see them again.

For a minute or so, Bill considered running the bunch back to his camp and into his horse pasture, but that would be a hard job for a man alone, and he could run his saddle horse down doing it. Besides, he didn't have enough grass in his horse pasture for the horses he already owned. All right, he'd catch one. That bay looks good. About eleven hundred pounds. Good head and shoulders and legs. Good feet. Looks like he could carry a man a long way.

Bill dismounted and tightened his saddle cinch. He mounted, took down his grass catch rope and tied the end hard and fast to the saddle horn. Let's go, old boy, he said to his mount, but easy. Let's see how close we can get before he takes off running.

The small band of horses trotted away. Stopped, watched him, and trotted away again. Bill got within a hundred feet of them, and believed that was as close as he was going to get. He squeezed the sorrel with his legs and held back on the reins at the same time, wanting to get the horse's hind feet under him, ready to move fast. The sorrel was ready, dancing nervously, knowing something was about to happen.

"Let's see if we can get on top of him before he knows we're after him," Bill said. "Let's go." Suddenly he slacked up on the reins and grabbed the sorrel with his spurs. The horse jumped into a dead run, hitting thirty miles an hour within three seconds.

The Indian horses snorted, wheeled and jumped into a run themselves. When Bill got close, they scattered, and Bill reined his horse to the left, after the bay.

"Sic 'em," he hissed. "Get after 'em, boy."

He had the loop whirling over his head to keep it open and to put some power behind it. The bay was no slouch and it didn't want to be caught. The race was on.

"Sic 'em! Huyah, huyah!"

The long-legged sorrel wasn't as quick on his feet as some of the short-legged cowponies, and he wasn't as good at out-maneuvering a cow. But when it came to a long run, he could leave a cowpony behind after three hundred yards.

He was running his best now, jumping gullies, dodging the yucca. His ears were laid back and he was running flat out. The bay had an advantage. Running free, it wasn't carrying a man and saddle on its back. And it was determined.

"Get after 'im, boy," Bill pleaded. "Sic 'im! Huyah!"

The gap between the two horses was narrowing. They were close.

"Another yard, old feller. Give me another yard."

Bill whirled the loop twice more over his head and pitched it overhand, like a man throwing a rock. The loop shot out. The honda, the eye in the loop, hit the bay behind the right ear and the loop encircled its head. Bill jerked the slack out of the rope with his throwing hand and picked up on the reins, bringing the sorrel to a slow stop.

"Easy. We don't want to jerk him down. Hope the sonofagun is broke to lead."

The bay hit the end of the rope, swapped ends and faced Bill, its nostrils flaring and its sides heaving. The sorrel was blowing hard too from the run. Bill got down and tied the reins to the rope so his saddle horse couldn't turn away. Then, with one hand on the rope, he approached the bay, not knowing what kind of horse he had on the end of the rope.

"Just stand there," he said. "Calm. Be calm." The bay had its head up and its ears twitching as Bill got close enough to touch it on the neck. "Just keep those feet on the ground."

Soon he was scratching the horse on the neck, then on the back, then under the belly. "You're a broke horse. A good one, I'll bet. How old are you? Will you let me look in your mouth?"

Moving slowly, Bill pried open one side of the horse's lips, then pried the teeth apart. The bay shook its head and jerked away from him. "Whoa, now." Bill pried the teeth apart again. "Uh-huh," he said, pleased. "A couple of cups left in those lower nippers. Seven or eight years old. A good age." He mounted, pulled the bay close to the saddle, wrapped the rope around the saddle horn, and rode away. The bay followed obediently.

The day wasn't wasted, Bill said to himself. I didn't find a homestead spot but I found a horse. That's better than nothing. He rode on a way and looked back. But I've still got the problem of finding some unclaimed water.

At first, when he saw smoke coming from his camp, he habitually reined up and looked for a place to take cover. Then, when he thought about it, he relaxed and rode on. The young squaw had a fire going and the stew pot simmering.

After taking care of his horses, Bill smiled a wide smile at her, one he knew she would recognize as a smile, and said, "Hello."

No expression. Only looked at him blankly.

"Feeling stronger? Sure smells good."

Not only did she have the stew simmering, she had some bread made—flat slabs of bread. She'd found a flat rock, heated it in the fire and fried the bread on top of it. Bill saw that she'd used some flour and baking soda, and...what else? He didn't know. Come to think of it, someone said the U.S. government gave flour and other groceries to the Indians in hopes of keeping them peaceable. She knew how to use white man's staples. The brown baby lay on a blanket a safe distance from the fire, but close.

Bill wondered if she knew how to cook Mexican beans. He dearly loved Mexican beans, and he'd bought a five pound sack of them the last time he was in town. Tomorrow first thing he'd get a pot of beans cooking. Maybe she'd keep them cooking while he was...doing what?

Thinking of that brought a worry frown to his face. Maybe he'd ride north toward the pine forest. He'd been told the pine forest was no place to winter cattle, but maybe he'd find another creek coming out of the forest that would lead him to good winter grazing. It was worth a try.

She was studying his face again, and damned if she didn't have the same kind of worried expression he wore. That made him grin. She reminded him of a dog taking on the same mood as its master.

As an experiment, he grinned broadly. "That little feller of yours looks fat and sassy." He tickled the baby's stomach where it lay on a blanket. The baby gurgled. Its toothless mouth opened in a wide smile, and bubbles of spittle spilled out of its mouth. "Doesn't take much to make you happy, does it." He glanced at the squaw.

First it was small twitch, then another, and then a quick smile. Bill had to chuckle. "How are you feeling? Stronger?"

No answer, but he didn't expect any.

They ate in silence. The stew was even better than the night before, and the bread was good too, even without anything on it. A right tasty meal and the kind that would keep a man strong. And that made him wonder again when the squaw would be strong enough to leave. She was eating heartily, using both a fork and her fingers. She would soon be ready to go. She had to. He couldn't keep her. Not an Indian. Glancing at her, he had mixed feelings. She was kind of pretty, with her high-cheekboned oval face, her black eyes and black hair. Her figure was, well, she was slender. Not a fat old squaw, but a young pretty one. And her breasts. Oh, Lord. He knew about her breasts. His hands trembled slightly when he remembered pulling her dress down and exposing them. Oh my God. He'd have to go to town soon and find a woman. A man wasn't made to live too long without a woman.

White men had bedded down with squaws. That wasn't unusual at all. But not Bill Williams. His brothers, if they found out, would never stop hoo-rawing him over that.

She finished eating before he did and stood. Stood straight. Straight and proud. Shoulders back and black hair falling almost to her waist. She had combed her hair. With what, he didn't know. Fingers, probably. It was as smooth as a curried horse's mane.

She picked up the dirty dishes and walked to the creek. Walked with her head up. Once, she staggered, but quickly regained her balance and walked to the creek.

Yeah, Bill thought, she'd be leaving soon. A wave of loneliness swept over him. But that's the way it had to be.

That night, before he could object, she took the blanket he'd slept on and wrapped herself and her baby in it by the fire. He opened his mouth to say something, but closed it again when he remembered she wouldn't understand. He looked back under the trees and saw his bedroll opened up so it would air out. Walking over to it, he saw the muslin sheets had been washed and were clean. The remains of some yucca roots told him she had used the plant as soap to wash the sheets in the creek. That's why most folks called them soapweeds, he reckoned. Probably worked as well as that yellow smelly bar of soap he'd bought.

He picked up the pillow and took it to her, but she refused it by shaking her head negatively. "Here, take it," he said. She wouldn't take it.

Bill Williams slept well that night. His stomach was full and he had his bed back. And no worries about Indians. They were gone.

All but one, that is.

The Indian bread with bacon made a good breakfast. She didn't care for the coffee, but he drank two tin cups full. She insisted, in her wordless, expressionless way, on taking care of the dishes. Bill agreed that washing dishes was woman's work. He opened the sack of beans, poured out about one pound in an iron pot and filled the pot with water. Her eyes followed him, and when he put the pot in the middle of the fire, a light of understanding came into her eyes. She knew what to do from there. Then Bill watered his horses and caught the bay.

He slipped the bridle bit in the horse's mouth and pulled the headstall over its ears. Then, picking up his saddle blanket, he said, "Let's see if you've ever carried a saddle." Hanging onto the ends of the bridle reins, he tossed the blanket onto the horse's back. Pleased that it didn't jump and throw it off, he picked up his saddle and lifted it into place. "Hell, you're an old broke horse, ain't you."

A glance at the horse's feet, and he allowed, "Gonna have to trim those hooves, though." He winched up the saddle, led the horse a few steps to see what it would do, then mounted. "Hell, I've got myself a free horse here. At least until somebody claims you. If somebody can show he's the rightful owner I'll have to give you up. But for a while anyhow, I've got another mount."

Riding up to the campfire, Bill dismounted, folded two slices of Indian bread, wrapped them in his duck jacket and tied the jacket behind the cantle. The bread would make a good lunch, and he was damned tired of missing lunch. He mounted again and reined the horse north. "Let's go see what's so terrifying about those woods up there," he said.

Turning in the saddle, he started to wave to the squaw and saw she was standing perfectly still and staring at something to the west. He looked where she was looking and saw riders coming.

They were white men, he could tell by their hats, and they were approaching at a trot. Just the same, Bill lifted the Winchester from the saddle boot and shifted his pistol holster.

There were four riders, and when they got closer he recognized two of them. They were the two who carried their six-guns low, tied down, the gunslinger types who rode for the Ladder.

CHAPTER 13

When they rode up, they sat on their horses without speaking. There were no greetings of any kind. Their faces were not friendly. Their eyes took in Bill, the camp and the squaw and her baby. Especially the squaw.

Finally, Bill spoke, "Morning." When he got no reply, he added, "Or is it?"

It was the broad-shouldered, bull-necked man who answered, "You're s'posed to be long gone."

"Yeah, well..."

"When're you pullin' out?"

"I'm riding, looking for a place. As soon as I find a place."

"And s'pose you don't?"

Bill shifted his weight from his right foot to his left. He met the bull-necked man's gaze. What he saw in that face, in all their faces, he didn't like and that riled him. Up to now he felt they had a right to this territory, and he was about to apologize for staying so long. But their threatening attitude got his dander up. "Listen, if you've got legal claim to this territory, I'll leave. But I'm not so sure you have."

"You heard what the land commissioner said."

That struck another sour note in Bill's mind. It was obvious they had talked with the land commissioner about him. And it was also obvious that the land commissioner had reported everything to them.

Now Bill's breakfast was sitting heavy in his stomach. A bitter bile worked its way into his throat. The whole thing didn't jibe.

Their horses were shifting nervously, but the four pairs of eyes held steady.

Another man spoke. It was the lanky Texan with the prominent adams apple. "Mr. Aarnstadt wants to know when you're gittin' out. He sent us over here to tell you to git."

Choosing his words carefully, Bill answered, "Like I said, if you've got legal rights, I'll round up my cattle and move on. But first I think I'll see if there's a lawyer in Colorado City. I'd like to see what the law says."

"About what?"

"A couple of things. Like, is it legal to claim a quarter section in any shape you want, and can you homestead land that hasn't been surveyed? I don't know. Maybe you're within your rights. But I want to see the law for myself."

The bull-necked man's words came out harsh, "You're a smartass trouble maker, ain't you?"

"I don't want any trouble. I'm a cowman myself, and I might feel the same way as your Mr. Aarnstadt. If I was here first, I might resent somebody else moving in."

"Then what're you doin' here?"

"I don't like the way this shapes up. I'm gonna read the law."

The bull-necked man dismounted and walked up to Bill. "I don't know nothing' about any law, but Mr. Aarnstadt wants you gone, so git."

Bill stood his ground. "When I'm ready."

"You want some help gittin' ready?"

One of the men haw-hawed. "He's got plenty of help. He's got a squaw. One of them young purty ones."

All eyes turned to the Indian girl then. She was standing still, wide-eyed.

"Thought we run off all the Injuns. He musta been keepin' that one in his bed."

"Yeah," another put in, "she must be good humpin'. Hey, Gar, you ever hump a squaw?"

"Haw-haw."

Gar didn't answer. He took a step closer to Bill. "Tell you what

84

you're gonna do, mister, you're gonna load your wagon and haul your freight out of here. And if we see any more of them Texas cattle, we're gonna drop 'em in their tracks."

He was so close Bill could smell his breath. The man had had a slug of whiskey that morning. A thought ran through Bill's mind: any man who drinks in the morning is a boozer, and no cattleman would keep a boozer on the payroll unless he had a special use for him. The special use was obvious. Gar was a professional gunfighter. Bill wanted to back up, back away from the man. His instincts told him to back away. He had to order himself to stand his ground.

In a fight it would be one against four, and they had come to fight. Back away, you fool. Instead, he ordered himself to look Gar in the eye, and he tried to put some strength in his voice. "You haven't got the only guns in Colorado Territory."

"Haw-haw."

"Whup 'im, Gar. Kick his Texas ass."

Bill didn't take his eyes from Gar's eyes, and that's why he knew the punch was coming and was able to rock back. Still, it hurt. It was a right-handed blow to the mouth, and it staggered Bill. Without thinking, Bill dropped his rifle and struck back, felt his right fist connect, but knew it wasn't a solid blow.

Another punch caught him in the left eye, and his vision blurred. He ducked his head and bored in, both fists swinging. One fist connected again, then another. Gar staggered back now.

"Jaysus Christ, Gar, whup the sonofabitch."

"Haw-haw. Want some help, Gar?"

Gar grunted with exertion as he began swinging wildly. For a moment the two men stood toe to toe, trading blows, hurting each other. Neither would back down. A hard fist caught Bill in the mouth again, and his lips went numb. A second later his right fist connected solidly with Gar's nose, and the nose spurted blood.

Gar was the bigger of the two and his punches were doing some damage. Still the Texan wouldn't quit. He doggedly kept punching, trying to duck under Gar's blows and connect with his midsection. Both men were breathing hard, grunting and bleeding.

Both refused to go down.

Then a strong pair of arms grabbed Bill from behind, pinning his own arms to his sides. A powerful right hand blow smacked him in the forehead, and for a second his knees sagged and he almost blacked out. Another blow hit him on the right cheek, then another in the stomach. With determination, he straightened his knees and pitched forward, trying to wrestle free of the man behind him. The man hung on. Another blow caught Bill in the cheek again, and this time his knees buckled.

"Hold 'im up, Goddamit."

"Can't. He's done for."

The man released his hold and Bill collapsed. "Goddamit, I ain't through with 'im yet." A boot toe caught Bill in the ribs. He was barely conscious, but had the presence of mind to roll onto his side, pull his knees up and try to cover his ribs with his arms. A toe caught him on the left arm and the arm went numb.

"That's enough, Gar. You don't wanta kill 'im." Gar was almost spent. His breath was coming in gasps. "Hell...I... don't."

He kicked Bill again.

"Don't, Gar." The voice had no authority and the lanky Texan was pleading instead of ordering. "Mr. Aarnstadt said to beat the shit out of 'im, not kill 'im."

The kicking stopped. Gar staggered to his horse, took the saddle horn in both hands and leaned against the saddle. His breathing was hoarse, and blood ran down the front of his shirt. "That sonofabitch. I ought...put a...slug in 'im."

"He got the message, Gar. He'll pull out now. Soon's he gets well. You fair beat the shit out of 'im."

Only barely aware of what was being said, Bill stayed in his curled position, wishing his head would stop swimming, wishing the men would leave. He was only barely aware of someone saying, "Aw shit, here he comes now." He was barely able to hear a wheeled vehicle coming, and he barely heard someone say, "He wouldn't give up, Mr. Aarnstadt. Gar had to teach 'im a lesson."

Gradually, Bill's head cleared. He tried to get up, sat down hard on the seat of his pants, tried again. He got to his feet and stood swaying like a drunk man.

"I half told chew, chew haf to go. Now mebbe you vill listen."

The voice sounded like it was far away, but soon the fat man's red smooth face came into Bill's view. He was sitting in his buggy, frowning at him. Sweat ran down the fat man's face. "Chew must be gone in a few days. Leaf. Go avay. I vill nodt tell chew again."

Bill said nothing, only blinked his eyes, trying to see better. His head hurt and his jaw felt like it was broken.

"Leaf. Understandt?"

His jaw worked, though painfully. With his tongue, he probed his teeth. They were still there. Next, he moved his arms. They worked. He took two steps. His legs worked too.

"Next time, squatter, I'll put a forty-four slug in your gut."

"Chust leaf."

The buggy team turned around and pulled the rig across the flood plain. The four riders followed. Bill stood drunkenly and watched them go. He watched until they were out of sight, then walked weakly to the creek, dropped to his knees and splashed cold water on his face.

Soft hands touched his face. Gentle hands. The young squaw was kneeling beside him. Her dark eyes were looking at a cut on his cheek. Her fingers fluttered over a bump on his forehead.

With a weak grin, Bill said, "Look like hell, huh?"

She stood and tugged at his shirtsleeve. "Huh?"

Face still expressionless, she tugged again, trying to pull him up.

"Want me to go with you, is that it?"

She tugged and pointed at his bed spread under the trees. Slowly, painfully, he got to his feet, went to the bed and lay on his back. She left, then returned a short time later with a bucket. Glad to lie still, he let her spread mud from the bucket onto his bruised face. It was cool, soothing. Her long black hair hung over him, and she brushed it back with muddy hands. He looked into her dark eyes. She avoided his eyes. But there was that worried frown again.

He had to grin. "If I looked like hell before, I'll bet I look downright funny now."

A smile flickered. Only flickered.

A cry from the baby got her attention, and she went to it. Bill just relaxed and looked up at the tree leaves. The meadowlarks were singing again, singing happily. Soon she was back, unbuttoning his shirt.

"Hey, wait a minute." He started to sit up. Gently, she pushed against his chest. "Well, I reckon you've see bare-chested men before." He lay still as she pulled the shirt off his shoulders and arms. Her fingers probed his ribs, and she smeared more mud on the bruises. It felt good and the pain went away.

While she worked on him, Bill's eyelids became heavy. Very heavy. At first he tried to force them open, then, with a sigh, gave up and let sleep take over.

It was mid-afternoon when he woke up. He was covered with one of his muslin sheets. His rifle lay on the bed beside him. His hands went to his face and found a thin layer of mud on his cheeks, forehead and jaw. The mud had dried and was caked. When he lifted the sheet he found his ribs covered with the same substance. It had a strange smell. Kind of sweet. Like the sweet clover that grew in the gulleys. He sat up. No one was in sight. He stood and found that he was sore, but able to move around.

A walk to the creek seemed like a long walk, though, and when he got there he knelt and started to wash the mud off his face. On second thought, after looking around again and not seeing her, he pulled off his clothes and lay on his back in the water, letting it wash around him. For a good fifteen minutes, he lay like that. He enjoyed the cool swirl of the water. Then he washed the mud off his body, off his face and out of his hair, and stood. That's when he saw her.

He hadn't heard her approach, had no idea she was there, but there she sat on the creek bank watching him.

"Gawdamighty," he said, grabbing for his broadcloth shorts. Hastily he stepped into them and pulled them up. She didn't change expressions, didn't look away, only watched him.

"How long have you been there? Why didn't you say something?" And then he remembered she was a savage and accustomed to seeing nakedness. Well, he wasn't accustomed to being seen naked by the opposite sex, and he was embarrassed. Quickly, he pulled on his pants and boots, then his shirt, and looked for his hat.

She stood, walked to where his hat lay on the ground, came

back and handed it to him. Still no expression.

"Thanks. And thanks for the nursing. What was it you mixed with that mud, clover? Whatever it was, it sure helped. For a while there, I wasn't sure I was gonna live."

Her mouth remained closed.

"Listen," he said, no longer embarrassed now that he was dressed, "I know you don't understand a word I say and I wouldn't understand a word you say, but you could at least try to talk to me. How about sign language? I've heard that you Indians can talk to another tribe with your hands."

No reaction.

As an experiment, he pointed to his mouth and moved his jaw. That got a reaction, but not what he'd hoped for. She motioned for him to follow, and went to the camp fire. There, she pointed to the pot of beans he'd put in the fire that morning. They smelled delicious. She pointed to his mouth and made chewing motions.

"Oh, well, come to think of it I am hungry. Those beans should have been cooking long enough. Let's try them." He picked up a spoon, dipped it full of beans, blew on them, then tasted them. "Good," he said. "Damned good. You know how to cook, don't you. You even knew enough to cut up some bacon to boil with these beans." Sitting on the ground, he ate a plateful and patted his stomach. "Good."

He was still sore, and he walked stiffly when he went to look after his horses, the bay had been unsaddled and turned into the horse pasture. She had put the saddle on the ground, on its side with the skirts and stirrup leathers straight, the way cowboys laid their saddles on the ground.

"You've got everything taken care of," he said, as he returned to the fire and sat wearily. "You seem to be fairly strong now, and that little kid of yours is fat and sassy. Now all I've got to worry about is me. What the hell am I gonna do?"

He shook his head sadly and glanced at her. She sat across the fire from him, keeping her distance. "I've got to do something, and I don't know what." A sigh came out of him, and he rested his chin in his hands. "There's one thing I do know. Those sonsofbitches will be back."

CHAPTER 14

He considered going to Colorado City and finding a lawyer or a copy of the Homestead Act. But when he looked at himself the next morning in the small mirror he kept among his cooking utensils, he changed his mind. His left eye was purple and the cut on his cheek was still raw. Not only that, he had several days' growth of whiskers, and when he ran a hand over his face he decided it was too sore to shave.

"I look like I came through a sick cow backward," he muttered. "People in town would think I'd tangled with a bear."

Not wanting to answer questions from the townspeople, he decided to wait a day or two in hopes his appearance would improve. Meanwhile, he'd get horseback again and go ahead with what he'd started to do the day before—when the Ladder men showed up.

The new bay horse was gentle, and he was glad of that. It moved out in a swift trot, and he headed north toward the pine forest. By midday he was there, in the cool ponderosas and lodgepoles. Anyone could tell at a glance that he was in an entirely different climate, and he wondered how the climate and the country could change so much in such a short distance.

Here, the grass was higher and of a different kind, and the wild flowers were everywhere. All colors of them. The soil was different too. Moist. It had rained here not long ago. It rained more often here. The tall grass was proof of that. Good grazing land. In the summer, that is. No matter how good the grass, it was no good for cattle when it was buried under a foot of snow. Horses could paw down to it, but cattle, with their split hooves, couldn't. Pretty country. Something about the woods made a man feel closer to the Creator.

What a cowman ought to do, Bill mused, was move his cattle up here in the summer and then move them south onto the dry plains in the winter. Damn, he muttered under his breath, if I could just find a good spot down there, this country is the answer to a cowman's prayer.

He rode on into the woods looking for a creek. When he found a good-sized stream he followed it until he found it going west, then south. He followed it south until he saw it join another creek that came out of the mountains. Stopping there, he looked downhill and saw a house.

It was a stone house, built of a material that was plentiful on the west side of the creek. A three-sided stock shelter and two corrals were behind the house. Horses grazed nearby. He counted eight of them. A well-used wagon road ran north and south along the creek. That had to be Fountain Creek which led to Colorado City, a creek that had already been homesteaded.

"An hour late and a dollar short again," he muttered, turning his horse southeast toward his camp on Owl Creek.

Riding at a steady trot, he got back at sundown, and while he was riding he wondered if she would still be there. She was strong enough to travel and go look for her people, and she probably knew where to look. In a way, it would be a relief to find her gone. He had no intention of setting up housekeeping with a squaw. But when he saw a spiral of smoke coming from the camp and his horses in their pasture, his spirits picked up a notch.

"Hello, Little Mouse," he said, as he rode up. "What's cooking?"

She was patting some bread dough onto her flat rock and she paid no attention to him at all. Not exactly the smiling woman happy to see her man return. Her man? Not likely.

Somehow she'd managed to make the beef more palatable, after he sprinkled some salt on it, that is, and the bread was better than anything he could buy in a bakery. With a full stomach, he took another look at the horse pasture, and knew he would have to move his horses in another few days. Hell, he'd have to move everything. Probably.

After dark, in the firelight, she pulled her dress down and let her baby nurse. Bill stared, wide-eyed.

"Don't you know you shouldn't do that? Do you know how long it's been since I've had a woman? What do you think I am, a Goddamn gelding? Goddammit anyway."

She didn't even glance his way.

In bed, Bill's mind went back to his brothers and their Running W Ranch just three miles from town. His older brother was courting a right pretty girl in town, and was always being kidded about maybe bringing a woman to the ranch. The younger brother had a girl in mind too, though she'd given no indication that she would consider being a rancher's wife. And Bill? He could only wish. Women were scarce in Texas. Women were scarce everywhere in the West.

Shaving was a little painful. He nicked himself twice with the straight razor. When he finished he washed the lather off his face and studied himself again in the mirror. Still looked like he'd been in a fight. Probably would look that way for a week or more. Well, he had to go to town anyway and read the law, or ask about it. He had to get this settled.

The sun was high enough to bring down heat when Bill put a crossbuck saddle on the dun and his riding saddle on the sorrel. The Indian woman watched him go, but showed no expression. He struck a trot and was well on his way when he topped a hill and saw a rider in the distance. The rider was coming toward him. Bill reined up and waited. When the rider got close enough, Bill recognized him.

Joel Hoskins.

They greeted each other in a friendly manner, and Bill appreciated seeing a friendly face. Hoskins still wore the soft leather shirt, now dark with age, and he still had his long hair hanging in a braid from under his broad-brimmed hat. "Looks like you're goin' huntin' or headed for town," he allowed.

"Town. About out of groceries. Where are you headed this fine morning?"

"I was comin' to see you. Heard you're keepin' a squaw."

Bill's eyes narrowed and he spoke guardedly, "Yeah?"

Hoskins reached for the tobacco sack in his shirt pocket. "None of my business and I was a squawman myself once. Thought I might be able to help you communicate with her. That is, if she's still there."

Bill said nothing for a moment, not knowing whether to believe someone actually wanted to help him.

"Not only that," Hoskins went on, "I thought I'd offer a warning. The word's all over town about you keepin' a squaw and they're sayin' you're squattin' on somebody else's claim. You're not goin' to win any popularity contest in Colorado City."

"I can guess who spread the word."

"Yeah. Gar Thompson. Cowboss for the Ladder. Says he beat the peewaddin' out of you, and from the looks of your face, I'd reckon you two sure as hell tangled."

"Not that I'm a fighter, or anything, but he had some help."

Hoskins twisted the end of his cigarette and struck a sulfur match with a thumbnail. "They're a tough bunch. Word is old Aarnstadt was sent here by some New York and Dutch investors to see that their investment pays off, and he hired some toughs to keep all others off this range."

"I can't blame him for not wanting other outfits' cattle around here, but I'm not so sure he came by this land legally. That's something I hope to find out today."

"I don't know nothin' about that." Hoskins smoked a moment, then, "If your squaw's still there and you want some help talkin' to her, I'll volunteer."

"Yeah," Bill said, turning his horses around, "I'd sure like to know more about her."

Riding back to Bill's camp, Hoskins told about living with the Cheyenne when he first came to Colorado Territory. He'd come to prospect for gold, but ran out of money and grub. On his way back to Missouri he'd shot an antelope to have something to eat. He was dressing it out when a Cheyenne hunting party came along. The Indians admired his gun, a Henry repeating rifle that worked sometimes and sometimes jammed, and offered him two horses for it. Hoskins allowed he needed the gun more than he needed the horses, but he shot two more antelope and helped the Indians carry the carcasses back to their camp on Sand Creek. They treated him so well that he stayed for six months.

"But then," Hoskins concluded, "some of them bucks got to attackin' wagon trains and takin' white men's scalps, and I wanted no part of that and I left."

Bill told about finding the squaw giving birth in the bushes and about helping her and bringing her to his camp. "She was so sick she couldn't walk, I couldn't just leave her there," he explained.

By then, they were back at Bill's wagon. The young squaw stayed out of sight until they dismounted, then she appeared from somewhere among the cottonwoods.

Hoskins faced her and raised his right hand, palm out. He said something that sounded to Bill like "Ya na." She raised her hand palm out and uttered the same thing.

Bill grinned. "I don't know what she said, but that's the first time she's said anything."

White man and Indian woman talked and Bill listened, not understanding a word. They talked verbally and with their hands and fingers. After a few minutes, Bill couldn't stand it anymore.

"What are you saying, what are you saying?" Half-turning to him, Hoskins said, "We're just making friendly talk now. I told her about living in the same camp with the Great Chief Flying Hawk, and about a few other Cheyennes I knew. We haven't got to the serious talk yet."

"Oh." Bill clammed up.

They might as well have talked Chinese. All Bill could do was try to guess from their faces what they were talking about. They sat on the ground, cross-legged, and Hoskins motioned for Bill to do the same. Hoskins rolled another cigarette, lit it. The talking and hand and finger waggling continued, and then Hoskins' face turned serious and the tone of his voice changed. Her voice changed too. Bill studied their faces looking from one to the other. She was shaking her head negatively and frowning. Hoskins was nodding as if in sympathy.

"What? What?"

She looked at Bill, talked to him. Her eyes pleaded with him to understand.

Bill pleaded too. "What did she say?"

"All right." Hoskins turned to Bill. "Here's the story." He paused to roll another cigarette. Frustration worked into Bill's throat, but he forced it down and waited patiently.

Finally, his cigarette going, Hoskins said bluntly, "Her man was killed in battle."

"Aw, no."

"But not with whites."

Bill grunted with relief, "Uh."

"He was in a huntin' party and he was killed by the Utes."

"The Utes?"

"Yeah. They're mountain Indians. Mostly friendly, but fightin' fools when they have to be. The Cheyennes like to hunt in the mountains in the summer, and the Utes figure the mountains is their country. They had a hell of a battle early last spring."

"Oh."

"Anyway, she said you saved her life and her baby's life, and she's obliged to carry out your wishes."

"No," Bill said hastily. "Oh no. She's not obligated to me."

Hoskins' face split into a wide grin. "Like it or not, friend, she owes you her life and she won't forget it."

CHAPTER 15

For a long moment, nobody spoke. The young Indian woman looked from one man to the other. Her face had gone blank again.

Finally, Hoskins said, "Wal, I've got to get back to town. Got me a stake and I'm gonna find the mother lode this time."

"You're gonna look for gold again? Where?"

"On the other side of that peak. Pikes Peak. The gold's there. Just a matter of time 'til some mother's son strikes it rich and it might as well be me. There's no call for wagon bosses anymore, now that the Indians've been run off."

Bill stuck out his hand to shake. "Here's wishing you luck. And thanks for coming out and doing my talking for me."

They shook hands. "Glad to do it."

Hoskins turned to his horse, stopped when the woman uttered something in Cheyenne language. "What?"

Gesturing toward Bill, she talked briefly, then waited for an answer. Hoskins talked back, grinned a wry grin, and talked some more. As before, Bill had no idea what they were talking about. Hoskins shook his head sadly, and that worry frown appeared again on the woman's face.

"Well?" Bill said. "What now?"

"She knows you've got trouble," Hoskins answered, "and she asked me what it was. She saw those Ladder jaspers beat on you, and she wonders why."

"Did you tell her?"

"Yeah. Why not? Don't know what she can do about it, but I don't see no harm in tellin' her." With a shrug of his shoulders, Bill allowed, "Reckon not."

After Joel Hoskins left, Bill sat on the ground and tried to decide what to do. Now he was known in Colorado City as a squawman and a squatter. Not the kind of reputation he wanted. If he could explain how he happened to have the woman in his camp, maybe they'd understand. Maybe not. As for grazing cattle on another cattleman's range, he hadn't known it was preempted or homesteaded or anything. When he first saw it, driving a big herd through, he'd been told it belonged to anyone who had use for it.

Now that he'd learned he was mistaken, he'd been intending to round up his cattle and move on. He'd been riding, looking for a place to move to. But dammit, they didn't have to beat him up. They didn't have to do that.

He glanced at the woman. She was looking away.

Standing, he began walking, eyes downcast, his mind on his problem. He unsaddled his two horses, turned them into the horse pasture, and resumed his walking. The woman watched him.

Down the creek, he walked, and back again. He grinned inwardly when he saw the tracks left by the Indians who tore down his camp the last time he went to town. Barefooted horses and moccasins. Just like the moccasin tracks the woman made, only bigger. Back again to the wagon. He sat on the doubletree where it was bolted to the wagon tongue and put his chin in his hands.

Suddenly, he stood and walked with hurried steps to the horse pasture and up to the captured bay. He'd already noticed the horse's feet, but he wanted to take another look. Yeah, they were rough, broken. Needed trimming. A horse's hoof was like a human toenail, if the outer wall wasn't trimmed every few months, it grew until it cracked and broke off. Bill hurried back to the tracks he'd been studying. The horses that had left them were barefooted, but had trimmed hooves. Next, he went to the spot where he'd fought off Indians one dark night. Moccasin tracks were plentiful, and farther out, away from the trees, more horse tracks.

Trimmed hooves.

Bill's horses were shod because he'd ridden them in the rocky country under the mountains, but cattlemen on the prairies didn't need to shoe their horses, only to trim hooves now and then. Indians didn't trim their horse's hooves. They probably didn't have the tools.

Now Bill was puzzled again. Again something didn't jibe. Why did the Indians tear down his camp and leave, then come back that night? Why did they come at night? If they'd attacked in the daylight, he wouldn't have lasted ten minutes.

"Goddamn."

Walking hurriedly, he grabbed a bridle and went to the horse pasture. Stopped, thinking. Not today. Tomorrow. It would be dark by the time he got to Colorado City today, and he had things to do when he got there.

Tomorrow, though, for sure.

The remainder of the meat he had hanging from a tree smelled a little rank, and he buried it out on the flood plain. He had enough trouble without getting sick on tainted meat. The young Indian woman managed to put together a good supper anyway. She used cornmeal this time to make bread and it was good. Added to that was the remainder of the Mexican beans and nearly all that was left of the bacon.

"I'll take the pack horse and bring back some more chuck tomorrow," he said. "If I can find some, I'll get some plum preserves to go with your bread. You'll like plum preserves." He knew she didn't understand, but he felt like talking. "If I can't get a quarter of beef, I'll go hunting. Antelope ain't bad if you know how to fix it. I'll bet you Indians know how to fix it."

Then his mood darkened. Here, he was talking like a man making plans for the future. Hell, he didn't know whether he had a future. He didn't know what was ahead.

"Dammit all anyway."

At first light he was on his way, riding one horse and leading another. His stomach was full of corn cakes wrapped around thick slices of bacon. The sky was clear and he knew the temperature would climb rapidly after the sun came up. Hot, but not as hot as Texas. Could use some rain. The rolling hills to the north and the flat plains to the south weren't as green now that the oat grass had ripened. Still good stock feed, though. The kind of grass that retained its strength after it turned brown throughout the winter. Boy, how he'd like to own a hundred sections of it.

The sky over Colorado City wasn't so clear. Kind of hazy. He guessed it was the steam engines that ran the sawmills, and the cooking fires. Too many people can mess things up, he observed. Two miles from town, a light spring wagon pulled by two horses came from the north and got onto the road ahead of him. He didn't try to catch up.

Colorado City was busy. Horseback riders, heavy freight wagons, buggies. As he rode past the stockade he saw that it was empty of people and wagons. The Indian danger was over. A new mercantile was open on Colorado Street and a new saloon was open across from it. At the livery barn, freight wagons were parked in a row, and the feedlot contained thirty or more big horses, the kind that pulled freight wagons.

"No feed for your horses," the livery man said. "Too many freighters goin' up Ute Pass to the goldfields." He was a short man with a wild beard and a cap with a bill on it. "They're growin' good hay on the creek, and I'm buyin' it as fast as I can haul it in here, but I might run short."

"I'm going back this evening," Bill said, "and they can get by without feed, but they ain't used to this city racket and if I tie them to a hitchrail they might booger and break loose."

"We-el, I got a pen you can put 'em in. You can water 'em out of that tank there." He nodded in the direction of a steel water tank in front of the barn.

"Good enough."

Horses off-saddled and penned, Bill stopped a bearded gent on the plank walk and asked where he might find the sheriff. "Lives over there under that bluff," he was told. "Frame house with a wire fence around it and some flowers in the yard."

But the sheriff wasn't at home. A woman who would have been pretty if she'd hadn't been eating too much answered Bill's knock on the door. She said Mr. Jenkins was over at the Colorado Warehouse where he owned a half-interest. Bill walked with spurs ringing the six blocks to the edge of town and found the warehouse on a well-used street. It had a long wooden loading dock, and two wagons were backed up to it. Men were carrying rolls of tarpaper, buckets of nails, and sacks of flour and sugar out of the building to the wagons. "He's inside," a man said in answer to Bill's question.

The light was dim in the big building, but Bill made out stacks of building materials and just about everything else a man needed to set up housekeeping, and he saw a middle-aged man standing beside a stack of flour, reading a sheet of paper. The man had a silver star pinned to his right shirt pocket.

"Are you the sheriff?"

"That I am." He looked at Bill over the top of wire-framed reading glasses. He was well-fed, with shaggy gray eyebrows and a short, trimmed beard. "And who might you be?"

"My name is William C. Williams, and I'm camped about twenty miles east of Owl Creek. I, uh..."

He was cut off. "You're the one that's squatting on Ladder land and keeping a squaw."

"Well now." Bill shuffled his feet, "I'm not so sure it's Ladder land, and I've got a squaw there because she was too sick to travel when I found her. What I wanted to see you about is, I believe somebody from the Ladder tried to kill me one night and make it look like the Indians did it."

The shaggy eyebrows went up. "The hell you beller. What makes you think that?"

"Hoof tracks. Made by horses with trimmed hooves. Not by Indians' horses. And they came at night when I couldn't see them well enough to identify them."

"Can't identify them, huh?" The eyebrows pulled together with a wrinkle between them.

"No, afraid not."

"I heard about you picking a fight with some of the Ladder's crew. They went to your camp and asked you kindly to move off their range, and you got mad and hit one of them."

"That just ain't so." Bill felt his face getting red. "In fact, that's a goddamn lie. They started the fight, and one of them held me while another pounded on me."

"You got any proof?"

"Proof?" Bill frowned at the wooden floor a moment, looked up. "How could I have proof?"

"Well, what do you think I ought to do, arrest somebody without proof that they committed a crime?"

Bill frowned at the floor again. "Is there a court here?"

"Yeah, we got a judge."

"I'll testify in court."

"Huh." The sheriff laid the sheet of paper on a stack of flour sacks and turned to Bill with his hands on his hips. "You'd be laughed out of court. And those gents at the Ladder wouldn't take kindly to you causing them so much trouble." The sheriff wore his gun high on his right hip. He was no gunfighter, but maybe he didn't have to be.

Anger pulled at Bill's mind. Anger and frustration. Of course he had no proof. How could he? Then an idea came to him.

"Is there a doctor here?"

"Yeah, we've got a doctor. Why?"

"I shot two, maybe three or four of the men who came sneaking into my camp that night. Anybody from the Ladder go to the doctor with bullets in them?"

"Nope. Doc Andrews tells me every time he takes a bullet out of somebody. Nobody from the Ladder has been to see him."

"Well, maybe they didn't say they were from the Ladder. Anybody go to him with bullet wounds in the past few days?"

"Yeah. Somebody's always getting shot. Two men were hit by the Utes five, six days ago."

"The Utes? I heard the Utes are friendly."

The sheriffs scowl deepened. "The only friendly Indian is a dead one."

"I'd bet anything they were two of the men who tried to kill me that night. And I'll bet there are a couple of fresh graves out at the Ladder."

"Now look here, mister." The sheriff took off his glasses. His eyebrows still were pulled together. "If you shot two men from the Ladder they'd report it to me and I'd lock you up. Matter of fact I ought to lock you up anyway 'til I find out what happened."

Bill couldn't keep the sarcasm out of his voice, "You don't need proof to arrest me, is that it?"

"Now see here, I'm the duly elected sheriff in this county, and I swore to uphold the law, but I didn't swear to take a lot of sass, and by God I'm not going to. If you've got no proof of any law-breaking, then you'd best get on out of here before I arrest you on suspicion."

Bill had to think, to fight down the anger that was beginning to boil inside him. Arguing with the sheriff was a waste of time and foolish. The sheriff had the law on his side. And he wasn't going to do anything to protect him.

"All right," he said after a moment, trying to keep his voice civil, "in case I'm found shot in the back, I want you to know what happened. They tore my camp down one day when I was here in town, and they came back that night wearing Indian moccasins and tried to kill me and make it look like the Cheyennes did it. But I was ready for them, and they got the worst of the fight, and then after the Cheyennes were wiped out or run off, they couldn't blame my murder on them so they tried something else. They beat me up and threatened to do it again. Next, they'll shoot me in the back."

"You're just running off at the mouth, mister."

"Aw, what's the use." Bill turned to go.

"What's that? What did you say?"

Bill ignored him and left, his boots thumping on the wooden floor and his spurs ringing.

CHAPTER 16

The sun was high and heat waves shimmered between the town and the blue mountains to the west. In spite of the heat, that peak up there still had snow in the crevices, white streaks running downhill. The mountains looked cool. Cool and mysterious. Bill stopped another man on the sidewalk.

"Pardon me, sir, can you tell me whether there's a lawyer in town?"

"A lawyer?" Bill hadn't noticed before, but the man swayed like a sheet in the breeze and his breath could kill a buffalo. "A lawyer? You want a lawyer?"

"Yeah, uh, excuse me. Sorry to bother you." Bill went on.

The man patted the six-gun on his hip. "I got a lawyer. Right here. Haw-haw."

Bill tried again. "Only one in town," he was told. This man was well-dressed in a gray vest, creased wool pants and spats. "You go two blocks west and one block north. On the corner."

"Much obliged."

He couldn't have missed the house if he'd tried. A four-foot high sign was nailed to a post in the front yard. ATTORNEY AT LAW. Bill walked up onto the porch, and his footsteps and spurs gave away his presence. The door opened before he could reach it.

"Come in, sir." Another well-dressed man greeted him, about his age, thick curly brown hair parted in the middle, and a thick brown moustache. "I am Amos J. Turnbull, attorney at law, at your service."

Out of habit, Bill wiped his boots on a straw mat and removed his hat before he stepped inside. The room had a braided rug on the floor, a rolltop desk and books, rows upon rows of books, lining two walls. Amos J. Turnbull seated himself in a swivel chair behind the desk and waved Bill to a wooden straight-backed chair in front of the desk. Bill sat, feeling uncomfortable, holding his hat on his lap.

"How may I be of service?"

"I, uh, I've got a question about the law. The preemption law and the Homestead Act."

"Umm." Turnbull put his elbows on the desk and made a steeple of his fingers. "And you are...?"

"My name is William C. Williams. I'm interested in homesteading along Owl Creek."

Turnbull straightened up suddenly and folded his hands on the desk. He stared at Bill a moment, then, "Well, Mr. Williams, the law is clear. All you have to do is pick a spot, build a dwelling, cultivate the land, and you get title to one hundred sixty acres after five years. At the end of five years, if you haven't made the necessary improvements, you lose your rights to it."

"Yes, I know that much, but..."

"Until that time, the land is yours for all practical purposes."

"But I've got a couple of questions. For instance, does the one hundred and sixty acres have to be a square piece of land or can it be in any shape I want it? And can I homestead on land that hasn't been surveyed."

"Hmm." The lawyer had to clear his throat. "You see, uh, Mr. Williams, such laws are passed in Washington, and communications between here and Washington are, uh, not very dependable."

"You don't know?" Bill couldn't believe it.

Clearing his throat again, Amos J. Turnbull stammered, "Uh, as I said, we here in, uh, the West don't always know what's happening in our nation's capital, and uh..."

"You don't know." This time it was a statement.

"Well, I don't have a copy of the, uh, law."

"If you don't, who has?"

"The, uh, federal land commissioner should have a copy."

It was becoming clear. Bill was wasting his time again. He

wanted to say something to let the lawyer know he was wise to him. He stood and clamped his hat on his head. "How much did they pay you?"

"Pay me? Uh, who?"

Without answering, Bill stomped to the door, yanked it open and stomped out.

His stomach reminded him he hadn't eaten since first light, but he didn't have time to eat. He walked the four blocks to the Land Commissioner's log cabin office and tried the door. Locked.

"Sure," he muttered. "Of course. Shit. Hell yes. I'll bet the government sonofabitch knows I'm looking for him and he ain't gonna be found."

Riding back to his camp on Owl Creek, leading a pack horse carrying full panniers, Bill knew he had as much right to that country, legally, as the Eastern conglomerate. Morally, he didn't. They were here first. But what rankled him was their way of illegally claiming the whole eastern end of El Paso County. And their bullying tactics. First a warning, then an attempt to kill him and blame it on the Indians, then a beating and another warning. What next?

He had no doubt it would be a shot in the back. Or in the chest. It would be a fatal shot no matter where the bullet hit. His body would be buried where no one would ever see the grave. In about six months one of his brothers would come to Colorado City looking for him. He would suspect murder, but he would have no proof.

The conglomerate, the Ladder, was pulling every kind of illegal, bullying trick there was to control a hell of a lot of grass. He knew it, the land commissioner knew it, the lawyer knew it, and the sheriff knew it. They all had Ladder money in their pockets. Bill was one man against many.

What to do?

His first thought was to fight it out. Keep a sharp eye just like he did when the Cheyenne were killing every white man they could catch. Hope to see the Ladder crew before they saw him. His Winchester would make them wish to hell they'd left him alone. There had to be a limit to how many men the conglomerate would sacrifice.

Fight the sonsofbitches.

He rode on, his horses traveling at a ground-eating trot. No, he couldn't win. They had the law in their pockets. They would shoot his cattle. He could retaliate by shooting their cattle, but what would that accomplish? They could shoot him and bury his body or lie and say he started the fight. If he shot them, he'd be arrested for murder.

He was a squatter and a squawman, and nobody would have any sympathy for him.

He couldn't win.

The young squaw had a stew simmering in the middle of hot coals when he got back. She'd cut up the remainder of the bacon and peeled some spuds and carrots and made a thick gravy. That and more cornmeal bread was all the supper any man could want, Bill thought. But he had a surprise for her. He's showed her the jar of apple butter when he'd unloaded the pack panniers and tried to explain that he couldn't get any plum preserves, but this was just as good. She didn't know what he was talking about. With a kitchen knife, he spread some on the hot bread and handed it to her. She smelled of it and looked at him blankly.

"I'll have to show you, huh?" He spread apple butter on another piece of bread and took a bite. "Hmm. Good. Go ahead. Try it. Good."

She took a small bite and chewed slowly, carefully. Then she took another bite and chewed faster. Another.

Bill grinned. "Good, huh?"

Looking at him, her face twitched. Twitched again. She smiled briefly.

"Say, you're taking to white man's chuck like a duck takes to water. Good, huh?" He nodded his head affirmatively, and his grin broadened.

Darned if she wasn't nodding too. Bill kept on grinning. Darned if she didn't smile again. Her teeth were white and even and strong and healthy.

He had another piece of bread and apple butter and ate until he was stuffed. When the baby cried, she jumped up and went to it. He took care of his horses and gave her the two cotton blankets he'd bought that day, and went to bed. His full stomach made him feel satisfied and happy—until he remembered he had to move. That brought sober thoughts.

All right, he could go either north or south. He didn't want to settle in a colder climate and have to fight snow all winter. That meant south. To the south was the desert. Nothing but sand, sagebrush and rattlesnakes, he'd been told. It takes about a hundred acres to graze a cow and calf down south. Well, almost a hundred.

He'd ride south. Take a blanket and enough chuck to keep him alive a couple of days and keep riding. Maybe he'd find some country that hadn't been seen before. Some good country.

Maybe.

At daylight, he got ready to go. No use trying to tell the squaw what his plans were. Well, he'd try. He held up two fingers, hoping she would read that as meaning two days. She only looked at him. "Two days," he said. He tried something else. Pointing at the sun, he said, "Two suns." No use.

His own bay horse was saddled, and a blanket with some corn bread and bacon rolled up in it was tied behind the cattle when he noticed she was gone. He looked through the trees for her and across the creek, then south. He saw her finally, carrying her baby wrapped in a blanket and slung across her back. She was ready for traveling.

Bill sighed and shook his head. She was leaving. He felt that he ought to say goodbye. Say something. Shake hands, or at least wave to her. She had stopped and was looking back. He waved. She waved.

"Goodby, Little Mouse," he said quietly. "I hope you find your people."

She was going south, so he'd go southeast, farther than he'd gone before. He swung into the saddle. She was still standing, waving to him.

Waving or motioning?

"What?" he yelled, and knew she couldn't answer. He watched her. She was motioning him to her. Puzzled, he reined his horse in that direction. But before he got to her she turned and walked on. He stopped. She looked back, stopped and motioned to him again.

"Well now, just a doggone minute." Touching his spurs to the bay's sides, he went on. She went on. He touched the bay's sides again and rode at a lope to her. "Wait a minute, will you. Where the hell're you going anyway?"

She pointed with her arm straight out and a finger extended. Pointed southwest. Continued walking, stopped, motioned him to her again.

"Oh, I get it. You want me to follow you, is that it?" Reining his horse in front of her, he said, "How far?"

She looked up at him, expressionless.

"How far?" he repeated.

First she pointed at the sun, then held up one finger.

"One day? You're gonna walk all day? And you want me to follow you?"

Side-stepping around the horse, she resumed walking.

"Hey, wait a minute." He caught up with her again. "If you think I'm gonna walk all day, you're crazy. And if you think I'm gonna ride while you walk, you're crazy."

She spoke then. For the first time, she said something to him. It sounded like, "Oh yo nah nah."

"Huh?"

She repeated it.

"Tell you what, Little Mouse. There's a better way to do this. You wait here and I'll go harness the team and bring the wagon. If we're gonna travel somewhere, we're gonna ride, not walk." With that, he wheeled his horse around and rode at a lope back to his camp. When he looked back, she was standing where he'd left her, watching him.

"Don't know what this is leading to," he said to himself as he hitched his Percherons to the wagon, "but I might as well go along with her. I sure as hell've got nothing to lose."

It took all day to get where she wanted to go. When he'd urged her into the wagon, she'd climbed into the back, behind the spring seat. "Not there," he said. "Up here." He motioned to her and pointed to the seat beside him. He did that twice before she shifted the baby to her bosom, raised her skirts, and climbed over the back of the seat. He offered her a helping hand but she didn't take it. When she raised her skirts he couldn't help seeing her brown feminine legs. "O-h-h," he groaned.

108

With Bill handling the lines and the Indian woman pointing the way, they traveled on and on over the flat grasslands, startling three small herds of antelope. Once, when they came to a deep gulch, too deep to get a wagon over, she pointed west, and he turned the team west.

Sure enough, they hadn't traveled three hundred yards when the gulch widened and shallowed out. She knows exactly where we're going, Bill realized. The country hadn't changed much. Still a lot of tall grass waving in the wind and some of the short buffalo and gramma grass. A little sagebrush. Lots of yellow flowers and some tiny white flowers. The farther they went the more sagebrush the wagon had to bounce over, but the grass was still good. In a sandy wash, a rattlesnake buzzed its tail. It was too far away to be dangerous.

Just before sundown, Bill reckoned they had to be out of Ladder country. Now if there was water...

That was when the Indian woman pointed southwest and seemed a little excited. "Where?" Bill asked. "I don't see anything. Not a tree or anything." She pointed again and smiled. For the second time, she looked Bill in the face and smiled. Still puzzled, he turned the team in that direction. Well, he'd been following her directions all day.

Another mile and suddenly he hauled in the lines. He looked at the woman and she smiled again. He stood up and looked ahead. His jaw dropped open. "What...? Good Lord almighty. Just look at that."

CHAPTER 17

He got down from the wagon. The young woman was right behind him, shifting her baby to her back. The brown baby didn't open its eyes. After walking twenty feet, Bill stopped again and repeated, "Good Lord almighty."

What he saw was a canyon three hundred yards wide and a good seventy-five yards deep at its deepest end. The canyon walls were every color that Bill had ever seen. The ground just dropped off. A man walking in the dark could fall into it. "Just look at that."

At the north end, the canyon dead-ended, and at the south it widened and turned into a shallow gulley. Looking down, Bill saw columns of clay with sandstone caps standing like sentinels on the canyon bottom. Just standing there. Also on the bottom were areas of thick scrub cedars and other areas of tall grass, the greenest grass that Bill had ever seen. A small stream wound down the length of the canyon.

The woman touched Bill on the arm to get his attention and pointed to the south end of the canyon, then pointed at the wagon.

"Think we can get the wagon in there?"

They climbed back to the wagon seat, clucked to the team and drove into the shallow gulley. Pointing, the woman directed Bill west in the gulley and soon they were in the canyon with walls rising straight up. When they came to thick scrubs and the stream, Bill "Whoaed" the team. The wagon could go no farther.

Still staring in awe at the canyon walls and the clay columns,

Bill whispered, "I've never in my whole put-together seen anything like that."

What he was looking at was the result of a million years of wind and rain erosion. It had exposed layers of iron oxides which had changed to brilliant colors. The wind and rain had also created a half dozen pockets in the canyon walls, three of them close to ground level.

The woman touched his arm again, climbed out of the wagon and motioned him forward. That was when he saw the foot path along one wall, through the scrub and grass. She followed the path and he followed her. When they came to one of the clay columns, she touched it, made a wry face, pointed to the sky, then made a quick chopping motion with her right hand.

"What?" Bill said. "What're you trying to say?" She touched the column, made another wry face and went through the same motions. She looked at him expectantly, then did it again.

"That rock is bad, is that it?"

The same motions again.

"You sure aren't scared of it." He thought it over, then, "Oh, I get it. Maybe I do. The rock is a bad man and your God turned him to stone, is that it?" He nodded affirmatively to let her know he understood. Or thought he did. She smiled and nodded.

"But how come all these colors? Man, the things old Mother Nature can do." He stretched his neck, looking up and all around. It was fast growing dark in the canyon, and even darker in the caves. "Good Lord almighty."

Again she motioned, and he followed on the path. She walked quietly in her moccasins and he walked noisily in his boots and spurs. They went past two small caves, and she stopped in front of a big one, big enough that a man could walk inside without bending over. Two steps leading to the entrance had been hacked out of the sandstone.

Hesitating, he felt as though he didn't belong here. This was a place the Almighty had created for Himself. He had no business here. But the woman went right in, stopped and motioned to him. Reluctantly, he entered. There were the remains of a camp fire, and the walls just inside were black from smoke. The interior was three times as big as the tarpaper shack he had built for himself.

The floor was littered with a broken arrow, a bow made of buffalo bone, short lengths of buffalo sinew, and a few strips of leather. Against one wall were three clay pots of different sizes, and against the far wall were two folded buffalo hides, tanned Indian fashion with the fur on.

Darkness was coming on fast, and Bill moved with quick steps out of there. "This is no place for a white man," he said. The woman followed, carrying a buffalo hide. They went back to the wagon, and, realizing they would have to spend the night there, he unhitched and unharnessed the team. If he'd had some wire he could have fenced off the south end of the canyon and kept the horses inside. But he had no wire, so he fashioned some hobbles out of the hame straps from the harness and turned the horses loose to graze. Immediately, they went to cropping the tall green grass.

"Tastes like apple pie, huh? You old ponies have a ball."

The woman had a fire going, feeding it branches broken off the scrub cedars, and Bill unrolled the blanket he'd tied behind his saddle early that morning and later transferred to the wagon. Their supper was the two rolls of cornmeal bread and cold bacon. Not filling. Definitely not filling. But better than nothing. The only light in the black night was put out by the small fire, and when the wind moaned down through the canyon Bill couldn't help shivering. A ghostly sound. Spooky.

Later, with the woman and baby wrapped in their buffalo robe and Bill wrapped in his one blanket, his imagination went to work. He imagined the canyon was full of ghosts of Indians looking for a chance to get even with the white-eyes. A groan came from him, as he put his hat under his head for a pillow, turned onto his side and tried to blot it all out of his mind.

The sun shining high on the west canyon wall made the world a whole lot brighter. Bill felt a whole lot better as he saw to his horses. Looking around again at the vivid colors and the stone sentinels, he decided the place wasn't so spooky after all. No ghosts had come for him in the night, and the horses were well fed and happy. The woman was up, but she hadn't built a fire. There was nothing to cook. He wished he'd brought more chuck and could do some exploring, but on second thought he'd have to go right back to Owl Creek anyway and take care of his saddle horses.

Come to think of it, why did the Indian woman bring him here? A place to live? That big cave over there had sure as hell been lived in. There was a creek and everything a man needed. A man and a woman. And a baby.

Aw come on, Bill Williams, he said under his breath, you're not going to keep house with a squaw and her baby. Are you? You need a place to homestead, but not here. Live in a cave? And though there's plenty of water for a few people, how about a few hundred cattle? Where does that water come from, anyway?

He took a walk by himself, gazing at the rainbow-colored walls, and following the stream. He walked to the north end of the canyon and saw water coming out of the ground. A spring. The water had originally spread over a dozen feet, but the Indians had dug a four-foot hole and let it fill with water. That created a clear pool where they could dip their water jugs, take a bath and wash clothes. Once the hole had filled up, the water spilled out and ran down the canyon. He followed it past the wagon, out of the canyon and into a sandy draw. There, it ran on for a quarter of a mile before it petered out, soaked up by the sand and sun.

If a man was to dig a hole in the draw, the hole would fill up and cattle could water there. In fact, with a team and a fresno, a man could dam the creek right here and build a small pond. Or...Bill walked out of the draw and into a gully. Here, the ground was grassy, hard-packed. It would hold water better. Yep, he decided, a man with a fresno and a walking plow could divert the stream over here, build a dam and water a couple hundred cows.

Excited now, Bill went back to the wagon and hunted up the woman. He couldn't keep the excitement out of his voice as he asked, "Is there any more water around here? Anywhere around here? Another spring, a creek, anything?"

She didn't understand, but she could sense the excitement and happiness in Bill's face, and she smiled, showing those white, healthy teeth.

"All right, let's go back to Owl Creek and move everything

over here. I'll go to town and get some tools and build a tank then round up my cattle and move them down here. Hell, Little Mouse, you might have showed me just what I needed to find."

It took two days to move from Owl Creek to the canyon, the painted canyon, as Bill was calling it. He let his Percherons rest while he stretched four strands of wire across the south end, creating a trap for the horses, a trap full of lush green grass. Come fall, he would have to build another, bigger trap out on the prairie, but this would do for now.

Early next morning he shot an antelope, brought it into the canyon and started to gut and skin it. Then he was aware that she was working right beside him, working efficiently. In fact, she was so fast with the knife that he just stood back and watched. In fifteen minutes she had the entrails out and in another twenty minutes she had the carcass skinned and lying on its back on its own hide. She took time out to sharpen the knife on a small piece of sandstone, then went back to work cutting the meat into meal-sized pieces.

Bill grinned at her efficiency. "I thought I knew how to butcher a beef or a buckskin, but Little Mouse, you beat anything I ever saw."

The team had rested two days. Bill hitched them to the wagon early in the morning, gathered the lines and climbed to the seat. The woman watched him wordlessly. He held up two fingers and pointed to the sky. She nodded.

They had learned to communicate at least that much.

As he left, he looked back for a landmark of some kind. It would be dark when he got back, and the canyon would be hard to find. There was no landmark, only the green-brown hills and a little scrub cedar. He looked at the sun and reckoned it would go down almost straight west. Colorado City, he reckoned, was west and a little north. Maybe more than a little north. Well, he'd do the best he could. He'd find it somehow. Pointing the team west, angling north, he looked back and waved. She waved.

"See you in a couple of days, Little Mouse," he said quietly.

He came to the wagon road about mid-afternoon. Traveling was easier from there into the town. Still, it was near dark when he pulled up to the livery barn. "Hope you can spare some hay and grain," he said to the bearded hostler.

"You're in luck. Had a whole string of wagons start up Ute Trail two days ago, and they left a little hay."

His horses cared for, Bill headed for the hotel where he'd stayed once before. The clerk, a bald, bare-faced little man in a striped shirt and suspenders, looked up from his newspaper when Bill came in the door. Looked up and squinted. The squint turned to a scowl.

"Need a bed for the night," Bill said. "A bed and a bath."

"Ain't you that Williams feller?"

The clerk's voice slowed Bill's steps. He answered cautiously. "Yeah."

"You're a squawman. We ain't got no room for a squawman."

"Huh? What?"

"We don't allow no Injuns in here and we don't allow no Injun lovers."

"What?" He couldn't believe what he was hearing.

The clerk's voice rose. "I said we ain't got no room for a squawman, and if you give me any trouble the sheriff'll throw you in the hoosegow so fast it'll make your head swim."

He believed it then.

Anger rose in him. It rose in his stomach and worked its way into his chest and into his throat. His face was hot with anger. When he talked he muttered through his teeth, "What the hell are you saying? Are you refusing to rent me a room because I saved a squaw's life?"

"That's exactly right, mister. Now git. Git before I holler for the law."

His throat was so tight with anger he had to force the words out. "And the sheriff, that piss-poor excuse for a sheriff, told you not to rent me a room. Or was it the Ladder? Somebody at the Ladder told you."

"Doesn't matter who. Git."

For a long moment, Bill stared at the clerk. He wanted to hit the man. Aim for his snotty nose and bring one up from his knees. Smash the shit-eating face. His mouth worked but no words came out. Hit him. Knock the hound dog shit out of him. He took two steps toward him. The clerk spun around and ran through a connecting door. Bill heard the back door slam.

It took a few minutes for Bill to bring his anger under control. That snot-nosed little piece of crud was going for the sheriff. The sheriff was just chicken shit enough to arrest him for something or other. Whenever there was a disagreement between a working stiff and a merchant, the working stiff got locked up. That's the way the goddamned law worked.

Get out of here, Bill Williams, he said to himself. You've got things to do, and you can't spend time in jail.

He turned and left, walking with boots *thumping* and spurs *ringing* on the planks. Where to go? There was more than one hotel. Sure, but whoever gave the order to refuse him a room had spread the order around. How about the cafe? No, the sheriff would be looking for him there. The mercantile, was it still open? He went down the street and across the street. Lamps on tall poles cast a dim light. The mercantile was closed. There had to be more than one mercantile, but they no doubt were all closed.

A saloon. There were plenty of saloons. One, just down the street, had *rinky-tink* piano music coming from it. Music and loud voices. Maybe he could get something to eat in there. No, the sheriff would make the rounds of the saloons.

Bill had met the sheriff before, and he knew the lawman was looking for an excuse to lock him up then order him out of town with a warning not to come back. The honchos at the Ladder wanted him plumb out of the country, and the sheriff would do his part. A man with a badge could do anything he wanted.

Well, it wouldn't be the first time he'd gone without supper. He went to his wagon parked beside the livery barn, wrapped up in the blanket he brought, put his hat under his head and tried to sleep. Tried to.

"Goddamn, Goddamn it to hell anyway." He'd wanted a bath, a meal and a woman. Instead he had a growling stomach and a hard bed in the back of a wagon. "Goddamn 'em all."

CHAPTER 18

Just before daylight, he crawled stiffly out of the wagon and tried to stretch the soreness out of his body. He could hear his bones creak. Thought he could, anyway. The gurgling in his stomach told him he'd have to eat soon or his belly button would be knocking on his backbone. He splashed water from a stock tank over his face, dried himself on his shirtsleeves and waited for daylight and the stores to open.

It was a cafe that opened first, the Ute Trail Eatery. Bill went there and stepped inside, wondering if he would be recognized. He took a stool at the counter, and no more than sat down when two other men entered. They were laborers of some kind. Sawmill workers, maybe. A middle-aged woman with a long flowery print dress came out of the kitchen wiping her hands on a white apron around her waist. The hand written menu tacked to a wall across from the counter contained the words Bill wanted to read: Ham and Eggs Twenty Two-Cents. Coffee Three Cents.

"Ham and two eggs over easy," Bill said, hopefully, "and coffee." She said, "Yeh," and went to the other two men. They ordered flapjacks and sowbelly and flapjacks and ham. She went to the kitchen.

Bill felt a pair of eyes staring at him, and he half-turned on his stool and returned the stare. "Say, ain't you the feller that's camped out on Owl Creek?" The questioner had a floppy hat and a four-day growth of beard.

117

"Yeah," cautiously.

"I hear you've got a squaw livin' with you. A squaw and a papoose."

Bill said nothing.

"Is that right? You shackin' up with a squaw?" The woman came back and poured three tin cups of coffee, set them before her customers and turned to go to the kitchen again. Bill picked up his cup, blew on it to cool it, and took a sip.

"Say, Elda, that there's that squawman we've been hearin' about. He's livin' with one of the murderin' Cheyennes."

"He's what?" She turned back and looked at Bill. "He's the one. Name's Williams. Ain't that right, mister."

Here it comes again, Bill thought. He tried to fight down the anger.

"Are you the one?" the woman asked.

"That's right." He looked her in the eye.

Immediately, she grabbed his coffee cup and jerked it away from him, spilling coffee on the counter. "I ain't feedin' no Indian lovers." She yelled into the kitchen, "Hey, Bert, come out here." A fat man came out of the kitchen, showing thick black hair inside his open shirt. "Yeah?"

"This here's that Williams, the one that's livin' with an Indian."

The fat man stared hard at Bill. "The hell, you say."

"Tell, 'im, mister," the woman said. "Tell 'im about your Indian woman."

The anger was rising. Bill fought it down. He stood. "Forget it. I'll eat somewhere else."

"You owe me twenty-five cents," the fat man said, hitching up his baggy pants.

"For what?"

"For a platter of ham and eggs and coffee."

"I didn't even seen any ham and eggs and I only got one sip of coffee."

"I got your order cookin' and I can't sell it to nobody else."

"I'm not about to pay for something I didn't get. You bring me my breakfast and I'll pay you."

"You're gonna pay. Oh yeah, you're gonna pay." The fat man

reached under the counter and grabbed a meat cleaver.

Bill's feet wanted to run out the door. The meat cleaver looked like the biggest, most dangerous weapon he'd ever seen. One chop with that could take off a man's arm. Or head. His feet wanted to run, but his mind didn't. That anger was rising fast.

The fat man came around the counter, holding the meat cleaver up.

Stopped.

Stopped so quick he almost tripped over his own feet.

He was looking into the bore of the big .44 in Bill's right hand.

"Take one more step, and I'll put a slug right between your stupid eyes." Bill's voice was cold, his face hard.

The fat man believed him.

Nobody moved. Bill's eyes went over the others in the room. Everyone was frozen. Finally, Bill backed toward the door. Slow. When he reached the door he turned and went out, his spurs *chinging*. Nobody followed him.

He was an angry man, walking with quick steps down the boardwalk. Other pedestrians stepped aside to avoid a collision with him. He was muttering to himself. "Now what? What kind of goddamn mess have I got into? Huh. I didn't do anything that I can be ashamed of. My brothers would have done the same thing. These people are full of shit."

At the livery barn, he paid the stableman and hitched his horses to the wagon, moving in quick angry jerks. The stableman watched him. "You mad at somebody, mister?"

"Not you," Bill said. "I reckon you haven't heard."

"Heard what?"

"I'm a squawman. I'm living with an Indian woman. My name's Williams."

"No." The hostler's face fell slack. "You're him?"

"The word's all over town, huh?"

"Yeah."

Bill turned to face him. "Tell me something, will you. Who's spreading the word?"

"Why, uh..." He backed up as if he was afraid of Bill.

"Who?"

"Why, uh, it was one of the riders from the Ladder told me."

"What's his name?"

"I, uh, I don't know his name."

Horses hitched to the wagon, Bill climbed to the seat. He sat there, trying to decide what to do. Would they sell him some groceries and tools, or did everyone in town hate him? He would have to try.

Clucking to the team, he drove out onto the street. He turned toward the mercantile and heard someone call his name. A man was walking toward him, grinning. A man in a buckskin shirt with his hair in a braid.

"William C. Williams," he said. "Even nesters like you have to come to town once in a while."

"Morning, Joel." Bill was glad to see a man he considered a friend, but he couldn't get rid of the tightness around his mouth. "Yeah. Looks like I wasted my time, though."

Joel Hoskins read trouble on Bill's face and stopped beside the wagon. "Got problems, huh? I know what it is. I only heard about it last night. Been up yonder and just came down."

"You got the word too, huh?"

"Yeah. They damn near wouldn't sell me anything at the Buckhorn Saloon 'cause I wear my hair long and wear this deerskin shirt. Had to do some talkin' to convince 'em my dust is as good as anybody's."

"They sure won't take my money. They hate Indians and anybody who lives with one."

"This town's got no love for Indians, that's a fact. Wouldn't sell you anything, huh?"

"No room at the hotel and no breakfast at the cafe over there. Had to use my six-gun to hold off a fat man with a meat cleaver."

Hoskins scowled. "That so?"

"Yeah, and that shit-for-brains sheriff is looking for an excuse to throw me in jail and lose the key. Hell, I don't know if I can buy some chuck and tools. In fact, if I was smart, I'd haul out of town right now."

"You can't fight the law." Hoskins scowled at the ground between his jackboots, looked up. "Need some tools and grub, huh? If you want, I'll go with you and do the buyin'. Maybe that'll keep you out of trouble."

"I never thought it'd come to this, but...well, I'd sure appreciate it. I'll give you the money to pay for it."

Hoskins looked up at the sun, then climbed to the wagon seat. "The mercantile over on Front Street oughtta be openin' up 'bout now. What kind of tools do you need?"

Bill kept his head down and stood by the team's bridles when Hoskins went inside the store. Hoskins came out twenty minutes later with a pimply faced teenager carrying one of the cardboard boxes for him. "Team's a little boogerish," Hoskins explained. "Has to keep hold of 'em."

On the way to a hardware store, Bill told Hoskins about the painted canyon and why he wanted a plow and a fresno. Hoskins whistled through his teeth. "Heard about that place. I didn't know if it was true. You've got to be the first white man to see it."

"Indians have lived in it."

At the hardware store, they used the same ruse, and it worked. A husky bearded gent helped Hoskins lift the long-handled plow into the wagon, and it also took the two of them to lift the wide fresno in behind it. Back on the wagon seat, Hoskins handed Bill the change.

"Naw. Keep it. You've earned it. You're the only friend I've got this side of Texas."

Shaking his head, Hoskins drawled, "Can't do it. Here. I've got some dust in my poke and I know where I can get some more. And I'll tell you somethin', I ain't lettin no mother's son tell me how to cut my hair and what to wear on my back."

"There's got to be some way to pay you."

"Naw. This'll blow over. Next time we meet you can buy me a drink of whiskey. Hell," Hoskins grinned, "we might even get over there and take on a couple of them ladies."

Grinning with him, Bill said, "I'm a booger for the ladies."

Five miles out of town, at a spot where he could see back down the road, Bill stopped his team and dug into one of the boxes of groceries. A sandwich made with a can of dried beef and bakery bread quieted his stomach, and he went on. At sundown, his team was tiring, and he kept his eyes peeled for a landmark. There was no landmark. At dark, he was worried. It was useless to try to find the canyon in the dark. A man on foot could fall into it, and though the horses had good night vision, he was afraid to take a chance.

"Whoa," he said, finally. "We'll have to camp here. And without water. Sorry, old ponies." He climbed down from the wagon and stretched his cramped knees. "I'm spitting cotton too. Wish I could find that place tonight."

He started to unhook the tug chains when, off to his right, he saw a light. At first he couldn't believe it. He blinked and wiped a shirt sleeve across his eyes. It was a light, all right. A fire. About half a mile away. He watched the fire grow. He grinned.

"Come on, old boys, she's lighting the way for us. We're going home."

CHAPTER 19

The team of Percherons didn't get much rest. Bill went right to work next morning plowing a deep furrow from the stream to the wide grassy draw. Hanging onto the plow handles, with the lines looped around his shoulders, Bill guided the plowshare and hollered, "Get up," and "Whoa," to the team. The furrow filled with water before he was finished, and he worked with his feet squishing inside his boots. By noon he had a ditch two feet wide and about the same depth. He had succeeded in diverting the stream.

When he unhitched the Percherons, he felt sorry for them. "All right," he said, "I've got a lot of riding to do. We'll put some of these other old ponies to work for a change. Besides, my hands and feet weren't made for a plow."

The Indian woman handed him a plate of Mexican beans, fried potatoes and a thin slice of antelope meat. It was good. After he added some salt, that is. How she had managed to make antelope meat tender and tasty, he didn't know, but she had. Almost as good as beef. Almost but not quite. Nothing was as good as beef, but antelope was free.

The rest of the day was spent horseback, and by evening Bill had gathered forty-two cows and three bulls and driven them to the man-made ditch. The cattle immediately put their noses in it and drank their fill. That made Bill smile. "Who says you can't improve on nature," he mused.

But, he admitted, as he sat cross-legged eating his supper, that nature's cave was a pretty good shelter. Wouldn't do in the winter, though. He'd have to build a cabin of some kind before cold weather hit. A one-room shack would do the first year, and he would add to it every year. This cave wasn't bad but...he glanced around carefully...in Texas a cave like this would be home to a bunch of rattlesnakes and a few tarantulas and scorpions and no telling what else. He wanted to ask the Indian woman about that but he didn't know how.

It was obvious she wasn't afraid. In fact, she was enjoying the meal, eating with both a fork and her fingers. Bill had to grin at her. She never used a knife to cut the meat, just bit it off. Her meal over, she took her baby to the creek and washed its bottom, downstream, not in the man-made pool where she drew water for cooking. The water was cool, even cold, but the baby didn't seem to mind.

Bill was tired. Following a plow was hard work for any man, and especially for a man not used to it. And he had a hard day's work tomorrow. Working plow handles was easy compared to working the dump handle on a fresno. He unrolled his bed in the grass by the creek, while the woman slept on a buffalo hide in the cave.

"Maybe rattlesnakes don't bite Indians," he said to himself.

Hard work is what it was. He hung onto the dump handle while the Percherons pulled, and the wide shovel of the fresno dug into the ground and scooped up dirt. At the spot where he was building a dam, Bill grunted and strained and raised the dump handle, unloading the dirt. Then he turned his team around and went back for another shovel full. It took most of the day to build a dam and scoop out a hollow about fifty feet long, but when he saw the hollow begin to fill up with water he was pleased. The foot work was done. Now he could get back in the saddle where a cowman belonged.

Tired, hot and sweaty, he stood beside the pool under the spring, and wished he had the privacy to take a bath. The woman was cooking, not watching him. He made up his mind, hurried to the cave, grabbed a bar of yellow soap, and hurried back to the pool. A clump of scrub cedar hid him from the cave. "Brrr," he said when he stripped and got in the water. Then, "Ahhh," when he got used to it. His face, neck and hands were burned a dark brown by the sun, and the rest of his body was white.

He lathered himself all over, ducked his head under the water and washed his hair, then lay back and let the water rinse him off. "Ahhh."

A splashing behind him turned his head. Oh, Lord. She was there. Naked as a jaybird. Splashing and washing herself.

"Uh," he uttered. "Uh..." He could think of nothing to say.

She bathed and stood before him, face blank as though she had bathed with men all her life. Pure female. Slender. Small firm breasts with little brown nipples. Small waist, belly button, hips that curved, flat stomach. And below that...

"Ohhh," Bill groaned.

Smiling now, she took him by the hand and led him to the cave.

He had it planned. By fall, before the snow flew, folks in Colorado City would have forgotten him. The town was the jumping off place for the gold fields in the mountains and it was growing. New stores were opening up. By fall he could buy lumber and whatever he needed to build a cabin. Until then, he'd live in the cave.

For the first time since he'd come back to Colorado Territory, Bill Williams felt good. He'd been riding for days and rounding up his cattle, separating them from Ladder cattle, until he had most of them grazing within a few miles of his man-made pond. They were fat but wild enough to make him glad he was horseback. Everything looked good.

Until he found the dead cattle.

Shot.

Four cows. Shot by Ladder riders just out of meanness. Goddamn. The goddamn sonsofbitches.

A bitter bile almost clogged Bill's throat. There was a small bunch of Ladder cows over there, about a dozen. He could knock down at least four of them before they stampeded out of gun range. Get even with the sonsofbitches.

Naw.

"Huh." Bill snorted out loud with sarcasm when he thought about going to the sheriff. That knot-head was on the Ladder payroll.

He'd find something to blame Bill for. What then? Go to the Ladder headquarters and confront that red faced, satchel assed Dutchman? Naw. It would be one gun against a half-dozen or more. They could kill him and claim he started shooting first. Besides, he didn't know exactly where the Ladder headquarters was.

Bill's shoulders slumped. There was nothing he could do. Just round up the rest of his cattle and move them southeast, out of Ladder country. He'd stay in his part of the world and those Ladder sonsofbitches could stay in theirs.

"But," he muttered to himself, "they'd damn well better stay in theirs."

When he saddled up next morning the sky was overcast, dark and threatening. A chilly wind blew across the plains. He rolled up a long yellow slicker and tied it behind the cantle, mounted and rode north. The clouds were so low he could almost reach up and touch them. A rain would be good, he thought. Green things up. He missed the sun, but he knew he couldn't have rain without clouds. The rain came with thunder and lightning. Thunder that sounded like cannon fire, and lightning that appeared to hit the ground too close for comfort. It was scary. Cattle and horses were a good target for lightning, and a man on a horse was an even better target. Stay off the hills, he told himself. Stay on the low ground, in the draws. But he couldn't find cattle that way.

He had decided to go back to the canyon when he spotted five longhorn cows, and went after them instead. Thunder boomed and lightning zig-zagged from the clouds to the earth. The slicker and broad-brimmed hat kept him dry down to his feet in the stirrups, and he didn't mind wet feet.

It was good to get back to the cave, though, where the woman had a fire going. He pulled off his boots and spurs, lay back on a buffalo robe and let the fire dry his feet. The woman lay beside him, and he let his natural urges take over.

The rain continued all night, but in the morning the sky was only partly cloudy and the sun was trying to come out. Mounted on the captured bay, Bill was pleased to see that some of the grassy draws held rain water. They would dry up between rains, he knew, but...

As much as he hated to even think about working with that plow and fresno again, maybe if he built more dams in the right places and channeled water to them from the slopes, he'd have more water tanks.

He had to try it. He was a cattleman, not a sodbuster. But he had to do it.

First, though, he had to find the rest of his cattle and move them off Ladder range. And that was what he was doing when he saw the Ladder headquarters.

It was an accident. He wasn't looking for it. But there it was. He'd gone back to Owl Creek, was following it west, farther west than he'd followed it before, when he topped a rise and saw the buildings below. He wondered why he'd never seen them before and then remembered that the wagon road veered south of Owl Creek. He'd never ridden west looking for a homestead spot because he knew all that country had been preempted.

"Well, well." He had to admire the buildings and corrals. A house where the Dutchman lived, no doubt, a bunkhouse and cook shack, a long, three-sided stock shelter, a small barn and four corrals. All made of rough lumber. Boards an inch-and-a-half thick. Cost money. Whoever built it expected to make a lot of money.

Bill turned his horse around and rode back the way he'd come. Not likely to find any longhorn cattle down there.

The sun was out as he headed back to the painted canyon. He was no more than a mile away when he saw smoke from the campfire. The woman was cooking something. The smoke drifted lazily out of the canyon and floated off into the sky. He was looking forward to a good supper and more love-making on the buffalo robe.

Then he saw the riders. Six of them a half-mile away. They had to be the Ladder.

Bill stopped and kept his horse still, hoping they wouldn't see him. But they too had seen the smoke and were heading in that direction. They were closer to it then he was. He touched spurs to the bay's sides and rode at a gallop to intercept them.

They saw him coming and stopped. When he caught up he could see the gunsel named Gar among them. Gar and the other tough-looking gunslinger. He'd hoped to catch them before they saw the canyon but he was too late.

The captured bay fidgeted as Bill sat his saddle and stared hard at the men. Then he said, "Don't tell me this is your range too."

"Our range is wherever we want it." Gar shifted in his saddle and returned Bill's stare. Then he nodded toward the man-made dirt tank. "What's that?"

"Just what it looks like."

"What's that over there? Looks like a hell of a big gully."

"Whatever it is, it belongs to me. The Ladder has no claim on it."

"Talkin' tough, ain't you."

"You're not what I'd call peaceful neighbors."

"How'd you like another whuppin'?"

"Who's gonna help you."

"Hey, Gar, let me have 'im." It was the other tough with the tied-down holster. "I won't need any help."

"Shit, this jasper's been whupped and it didn't do no good. There's only one language a squaw-humpin' claim jumper like him understands."

The six-gun appeared in Gar's right hand so fast that Bill didn't even know he was reaching for it. His own pistol was still riding on his left hip, butt forward.

Someone laughed. "Haw-haw."

A chill swept over Bill as he looked into the bore of Gar's six-gun. His breath turned to ice. Even the captured bay stood still.

"Git down."

"Why?" The word was a gasp.

"'Cause I said so. When I holler frog, you jump, savvy?"

Bill looked each man in the eye. The thin galoot with the prominent adams apple couldn't meet his gaze.

"Git down or I'll shoot you down."

He was as good as dead. There were six of them, all armed with pistols and rifles. If he were a professional gunfighter he might get one or two, but the others would get him. And he was no gunfighter. With a crooked sheriff on the Ladder's payroll, they would kill him and get away with it.

Well, by God, he was going down fighting. If he got off his

horse and Gar stayed horseback, he might get lucky. Gar's horse could spook and spoil his aim, while Bill would be in a better position to shoot. Heart pounding, he slowly dismounted. He watched Gar's horse.

"Hey, Gar, lookee there." It was the thin galoot, pointing at Bill's captured bay. "Look, that horse ain't got no brand."

Gar's eyes never left Bill's gun hand, and he spoke out of the side of his mouth, "Yeah, so what?"

"So it's a stole horse, that's what. And Ah'll bet Ah know who it was stole from."

"Yeah, who?"

"A gentleman name of Pritchard. Milks a bunch of cows north of Colorado City and breeds some mares. Morgans is what he calls his stud. That horse is a half-breed."

"You sure about that, Tex?"

"Damn right Ah'm sure."

"Shuck your gun." The order was directed at Bill. Again, Bill looked at each man. This time Tex met his gaze. If he dropped his gun he would have no chance at all. His mind raced, trying to decide what to do.

"They hang horse thieves, Gar. We don't havta kill this Tejano. The law'll do it for us."

"Yeah, that's right." Gar's face brightened. "That's the best way. Turn 'im over to the law." To Bill he said, "Shuck your gun, and I mean right now. We can shoot you for a thief right here or you can go to town and take your chances."

That was an easy decision. If he tried to shoot it out he'd die on the spot. In town, all he had to do was get Pritchard or whatever his name was to tell the sheriff and everybody else that the horse was stolen by Indians. He started to argue with the men, tell them how he happened to have the horse, but changed his mind. Tell his story in town, not here.

He unbuckled his gunbelt and let it drop. The galoot named Tex got down, picked up the belt, gun and all, buckled it together and hung it over his saddle horn.

"I oughta make you walk," Gar said.

"Shit, Gar, if he walks we'll be all night gittin' to town."

"Git on your horse." Suddenly Gar haw-hawed. "Git on your stole horse."

A rider lifted Bill's Winchester from the saddle boot before Bill got mounted. Then, unarmed and surrounded by six heavily armed men, Bill turned his horse toward town. Looking back at the painted canyon, his heart sank into his stomach. Wait for me, Little Mouse, he said under his breath.

CHAPTER 20

Just before dark, Gar took the short braided rope that Bill always carried under the back rigging rings of his saddle, and tied his hands behind his back.

"That's in case you think about gettin' away in the dark."

Bill snorted. The rope was for tying down cattle and now it was tying him. With his hands behind his back and someone leading his horse he'd never felt so helpless.

They rode into town long after dark and had to get sheriff Ben Jenkins out of bed. He came out of the house grumbling and buckling his belt. He wore no shirt except for a cotton undershirt. Holding a lantern up to Bill's face, he swore. "Goddamnit to hell, I should've locked you up the first time I saw you. Goddamnit, I knew you were trouble. First you try to take over somebody else's land, then you start shacking up with the goddamn Indians, and now you're stealing horses."

In the dim lamplight, Bill could see the sheriff's shaggy eyebrows waggling like the antennae on a cockroach. He started to protest, then changed his mind and kept his mouth shut.

At the one-room jail, they went through his pockets, took his folded paper money and his pocket knife. "I know exactly how much money I've got there," Bill said. "A hundred and fifteen dollars. I want it back. Every cent."

"I've got a hunch," the sheriff said, "you won't ever spend another cent. We'll make you pay for the rope we hang you with."

Someone haw-hawed.

They untied his hands before they shoved him into the jail. Knocked him inside, that is. Just as his hands were untied, one of the men, he didn't see which one in the dark, hit him in the face. He staggered backward. The door slammed shut.

Rubbing his wrists to get the blood circulating, he stood still in total darkness and whispered, "Anybody in here?" No sound. He whispered again. He was alone. With his hands, he found a wall and sat on the splintery wooden floor with his back to it.

There was no sleeping. After a while he got up and used his fingers to grope the inside of the building, the door, the hinges, everything. The room was completely empty except for him. If there was a way to break out he couldn't find it in the dark. He didn't want to break out anyway. Tomorrow he'd be taken before a judge and he would explain how he happened to be riding that horse. They'd find the owner and the owner would tell the judge how he'd lost the horse. And they would have to set him free. That was better than breaking out.

When daylight slowly crept in through the one narrow window, he was wide awake. Now he could see that the jail was built of heavy timbers, bolted together. The floor was the same.

By standing on his toes he could see out the window. The street was alive with wagon and horseback traffic, and he could hear men's voices. Tiring of that, he sat on the floor again and waited. It was two hours before he heard another human voice, and the voice he heard was young. Very young.

"There's s'posed to be somebody in there," the voice said. "Hold me up." A youthful face with a ragged bill cap over it appeared in the window. "Hey," it said, "there is somebody in there." The face disappeared.

Another youthful voice said, "Let me look. Let me stand on your back." A different face appeared, young, tow-headed. "Hey, mister, what'd you do? Are you a robber?"

"Naw," Bill said, and he put his face in his hands.

He didn't feel like talking.

An hour later, the door opened, slowly. Two men stood outside with six-guns in their hands and the hammers back. Another man came in with a galvanized bucket. "You can use this for a toilet," he said, setting the bucket on the floor.

"When do I get to see the judge?" Bill asked.

"Whenever Mr. Jenkins says so."

"Where is the sheriff?"

"He's got some business to take care of."

"Sure he has." Bill couldn't keep the sarcasm out of his voice.

"We'll bring you some breakfast in a minute."

Breakfast was two cold pancakes and a cold cup of coffee. Bill ate the pancakes and ignored the coffee. At noon, his stomach told him it was time to eat again, but no noon meal was brought to him.

Voices outside the window again. More kids. "Let me see." Another boyish face with freckles and a shock of blond hair over the forehead. "Yeah, he's in there." Then another face. "Hey, mister, did you rob somebody?"

Bill walked over to the window. "I didn't rob anybody. Do you know a farmer named Pritchard?"

"I've heard of Zeke and Luke Pritchard."

"Brothers?"

"Yeah."

"Where do they live?"

"Up north. Toward Denver."

"How far?"

"I think it's, uh, three miles. Mebbe four. I ain't never been there. I only heard about 'em."

"How can I get there?"

"On the stage road to Denver, that's all I know. Why? You mad at 'em?"

"No. I'm not mad at anybody."

"You shoot somebody?"

"Naw."

"Come on, Will, it's my turn."

Then a man's voice, "Hey, you kids. Git away from there. Git away from there before I lock you up too."

It was nearly dark when they brought him his supper: mashed potatoes, no gravy, a piece of tough meat. Tasteless. He had to force himself to chew and swallow. When they came for the empty plate, he asked the same question and got the same answer. "I've heard there's a judge in town. When do I get to see him?"

"Whenever Mr. Jenkins says so."

He reckoned it was about midnight when he heard whispers outside the door.

There were at least two men. They whispered, and then they were quiet. Bill stood by the door, waiting to see what was going to happen. He heard a key in the large padlock, then heard the door swing slowly open. Then quiet. Bill breathed with shallow breath and waited. Nothing happened.

All he could see outside was a lamplight across the street. The night in front of the jail was black. He waited, breathing as little as possible. Nothing.

Something was wrong. They didn't open the door by mistake. They wanted him out. Uh-oh. Now he got it. They wanted him to run so they could shoot him and say he was shot trying to escape. What would happen if he didn't run? Would they drag him out and shoot him? Yeah. They wanted him dead. Either way, they intended to kill him.

Think, Bill Williams, he told himself. You've got to do something. What? Think.

Desperate now, he hit upon a plan. It wouldn't work, but he had to try.

He took off his spurs, took the slop bucket by the handle, backed up to the far end of the room, clenched his jaws, took a deep breath and ran.

Heavy boots clomped on the wooden floor as Bill ran to the door. But at the door he stopped and threw the bucket out into the yard. Someone yelled, "Git 'im," and two six-guns fired almost at once. Gunflashes showed Bill there was a gun on each side of the door. He grabbed at the one on the right, got a man's arm, yanked, pushed, twisted.

The man yelled, "Here he is. Come git the sombitch off me."

Bill had the gun then, and had a finger between the hammer and the bullet. He twisted, kicked with his boots and his knee and butted with his head. The gun came free.

"Git 'im. Git the sombitch."

Holding the gun by the barrel, Bill swung it in a wide arc. It collided with the man's head. Bill swung again. Then he ducked around a corner of the building, headed for the darkest spot he could see and ran.

A gun fired, and he heard the bullet zing past his ear. More shots. He ran, stumbled over something in the dark, regained his balance and ran.

The shooter was firing at the sound now, but Bill couldn't help making a noise. He cut sharply to the right and ran toward the outskirts of town.

The gunfire ceased, but the heavy footsteps were coming his way. He heard a man stumble and curse. On he ran until his breath was coming in ragged gasps. When he found himself running across a vacant lot in tall weeds, he stopped and dropped onto his hands and knees. The footsteps were going to his left. They didn't know where he was. Bill panted and gasped. Dogs were barking, but they were all over town and none gave away his position. The six-gun was still in his right hand. He stayed on his hands and knees until his breathing returned to normal, then stood up and walked as quietly as he could down alleys, out to the edge of town, and on out onto the dark plains.

When he was far enough from town that he felt safe, he sat on the ground and let the cool night wind blow over him. All that running and walking had made his feet sore and his legs ache. He'd lost his hat when he'd fought with the unseen man at the jail, and he missed it. He always felt undressed without a hat. The night wind was soothing. He lay back and looked up at the stars.

He'd heard of people who swore they could predict the future by studying the stars. "Huh," he snorted out loud. Maybe he didn't want to know about the future. Right now his future didn't look too bright. He did wish the stars would tell him what to do about it. "What?" he said.

And it came to him. Sure. There was only one thing he could do. As soon as it was daylight.

CHAPTER 21

He was walking north, paralleling the stage road, but staying far enough away that he could drop out of sight if he saw anyone coming from Colorado City.

Three or four miles, the kid had said. But the kid admitted he really didn't know.

About two miles north of town he saw a farm with a log house and barn and a field of vegetables of some kind. A man, woman and a boy were working on their hands and knees in the field. He switched directions and started over there, then stopped. The six-gun was stuck inside his belt. He knew that if he approached the farmers carrying a gun that way, they'd be suspicious. He hated to give up the gun. He might need it. But he needed directions more. He dropped the gun on the ground. "Morning," he said when he got close enough, forcing cheerfulness.

Their heads jerked up, surprised.

"I'm looking for the Pritchard place."

They all stood, and they stood with their knees bent as if they'd been in that position a long time. What was that crop? Cabbage? Their eyes went over him, from his bare head down to his riding boots.

Finally, the man spoke, "The Pritchards?"

Smiling as pleasantly as he could, Bill answered, "Yes sir."

He could tell they wanted to know why he was looking for the Pritchards, but didn't want to ask. He didn't volunteer anything. "About two mile straight north. On the crik. Big white house. Can't miss it."

His feet felt like one big boil and his legs were weak by the time he got to the big white house. Not only that, his stomach was complaining about the shortage of food. Bill walked into the yard, surrounded by a plank fence with flowers along the fence. A woman's touch. Two horses stood in a corral east of the barn. A dog ran at him barking, but wagging its tail. Another horse, a bay, stood in another pen. A pretty one, with long mane and tail, proud head and neck. A stud.

White frame house. Lacy curtains in the windows. Another woman's touch. The woman heard the dog barking and came out on the porch. Her eyes widened when she saw him.

Forcing another smile, Bill said, "Morning, ma'am. Is this the Pritchard farm?"

A pleasant-looking woman, though a little work worn. Plump, with gray hair knotted behind her head. "Yes, it is."

"Is Mr. Pritchard at home?"

"Which one?"

"Either one, ma'am. I want to talk to him about a horse."

"He's out to the barn. I'll call him." She stepped off the porch, looked toward the barn, cupped her hands around her mouth and let out a yell that would make any cowboy proud of himself. "E-e-ze- e-ki-e-l."

A man in a straw hat and bib overalls came out of the barn. He saw Bill and walked toward the house.

"Are you Mr. Pritchard?" Bill asked when the farmer was close enough.

"I am."

"Mr. Pritchard...my name is Bill Williams." He paused to see if his name got a reaction. The farmer raised a questioning eyebrow, but said nothing. Bill cleared his throat and went on. "Mr. Pritchard, I've been accused of stealing a horse that somebody said belongs to you."

Both eyebrows went up. Man and woman were staring at Bill.

"He's a bay gelding. About eleven hundred. Good looking horse. Looks a lot like that horse over there."

"Where'd you find 'im?"

"About thirty miles east. A little way north of Owl Creek. He was running with some Indian horses."

"See any more like 'im?"

"No sir. The horses he was running with looked like mustangs."

"Where's he at now?"

"Sheriff Jenkins has him now, I, uh, after I caught him, I, uh, I've got some cattle over there and I needed another horse and I rode him. I knew he belonged to somebody and I knew I'd have to give him up when the rightful owner claimed him. I had no intentions of keeping him."

The woman spoke then, "And the sheriff thinks you stole him."

"Yes, ma'am."

"He was stole, all right," the farmer said, "but not by you. It was the Cheyennes. My brother and I saw 'em. They run off four of my good geldings. We went after 'em a way, but when we got close we saw there was about a dozen of them Indians and they all had long guns."

Bill's smile was genuine then. "You don't know how happy I am to hear you say that, Mr. Pritchard. I hope you don't hold it against me for riding your horse. I didn't mistreat him, and he's in good shape."

"You say the sheriffs got 'im? Wal, I'll have to go git 'im. I'd sure like to find, the rest of 'em."

"Uh, Mr. Pritchard, I have to ask something of you. I need you go to town and tell everybody how you lost that horse. Not just the sheriff, but everybody. Everybody you know."

"Mr. Williams," the woman said, "if the sheriff thinks you stole a horse why aren't you in that jail they've got?"

"I was, ma'am. They didn't give me a chance to explain anything. I ran."

"Oh?" Her eyes widened.

"I'll hitch up a team to the buckboard," the farmer said.

They attracted attention as soon as they turned onto Colorado Street. Everyone had heard about the jail break. "Is that him? How'd you ketch 'im, Zeke?"

"He's a hoss thief, Zeke. Take 'im over to the jail."

By the time they got to the sheriff's house some twenty

townsmen, women and kids were walking along behind. Sheriff Ben Jenkins wasn't at home, but someone had gone for him, and he soon appeared, puffing from hurrying. He no more than saw Bill than he drew his six-gun.

"All right, get down from the wagon before I shoot you down," he said.

Bill kept his seat.

"I'm warning you."

The farmer spoke, "Wait a minute now, sheriff. This man's got a story to tell and I think he ought to be allowed to tell it."

"Well, I've got a story to tell too. He broke out of jail last night. Waited 'till my helpers went to give him some supper, hit one over the head, took his gun and ran."

Bill climbed down from the wagon then, stood in front of the sheriff and spoke through his teeth, "That's a lie."

The six-gun in the sheriff's hand was raised, and Bill found himself looking down the bore. A murmur went through the crowd. "What was that? What was that you said?"

"Now Ben." Zeke Pritchard stood in the wagon and raised his voice. "This man came to me and told me he was accused of stealing a horse from me. The only ones that stole from me was the Cheyennes. If he's got one of my horses he got it from the Indians or found it runnin' wild with the Indian horses like he said."

"That ain't what he told me," the sheriff said. Bill's jaws were still so tight from anger that he could barely talk, and he hissed, "I didn't tell you anything. Telling you anything is like talking to a rock. Why didn't you let me see the judge?"

"I would have if you hadn't broke out of jail."

"They came for me at midnight, and they were going to shoot me and make it look like I tried to bust out. You sent them."

"That's a lie. You're a liar."

With clenched teeth, Bill said, "Why don't you put that gun down and call me that."

"I'm a duly elected officer of the law, and..."

The farmer interjected, "Where is the horse? Let me see the horse he was s'posed to of stole."

"He's over in the livery barn," a man in the crowd said. "I'll fetch 'im."

It was only minutes, but to Bill it seemed like hours. Someone in the crowd said, "We don't need a judge to hang a horse thief." Another said, "He's that squawman. He lives with an Injun." The sheriff's gun was lowered a few inches, but it still was aimed at Bill's chest. Finally, the horse was led up.

"That's my horse," the farmer said. "That's one of four that was run off by a bunch of savages. I saw 'em, my brother and me, but there was too many of 'em."

The sheriff's gun didn't waver. "He was caught riding that horse."

"Wal, Ben, if he hadn't roped that horse I wouldn't be gittin' 'im back. He didn't hurt 'im none. I ain't complainin'."

"But he broke out of jail." Ben Jenkins' voice didn't carry quite as much authority now.

"Listen here," Zeke Pritchard looked over the crowd, "this man came to me and told me what happened. He could of been half way to Denver by now. I don't think he done anything wrong."

"Well," the sheriffs voice was even weaker, "you can't blame me for locking him up 'til I found out what happened. That's what you all elected me for."

"You done your job, shurff," someone said.

"Do we haveta let 'im go?"

Ben Jenkins holstered his six-gun. "You can go."

"Not yet," Bill said. "You took everything out of my pockets, including my money. I want it back." Looking up at his wife standing on the porch, Ben Jenkins said, "It's in that cigar box on my desk." She went into the house and returned in a few minutes.

Bill counted the money, folded it, put it in his shirt pocket and buttoned the pocket. "You've got my guns too. Get my guns."

Mrs. Jenkins made another trip into the house and came back carrying Bill's holstered six-gun, his Winchester, and cartridge belt. Bill buckled it around his waist. The gun was on his left hip, butt forward. Then he turned the belt around so the gun was on his right hip. He loosened the belt a notch, allowing the gun and holster to hang lower. Now he faced the sheriff, his face hard and his eyes slits. "You want to call me a liar again?" His right hand hovered over the gun butt.

"Huh? What?" the sheriff could only sputter.

"It's different when you're facing an armed man, ain't it, law dog."

The sheriff said nothing, and made no move toward his gun either. Someone else spoke, "You'd better git, mister. You're lucky you ain't swingin' from a tree."

"Yeah, you'd better git."

For a long moment, Bill's eyes dared the sheriff to move. Finally he looked away. When he spoke again, his voice was softer. "Uh, Mr. Pritchard, I sure do appreciate your help. I'm much obliged. Tell your missus I'm obliged to her too."

Then, looking over the crowd, he said, "The rest of you can go to hell."

"What? What did he say?"

"Let me at that sombitch."

Bill walked through them, determined to make them step aside. His face was hard again. He looked straight ahead. They got out of his way.

CHAPTER 22

He walked to the livery barn, stopping on the way at the land commissioner's office. Locked, of course. He found his saddle and his hat, bought a gray horse that had been overworked and underfed, and paid the stableman too much for it. Well, he needed another horse, and this one was only six years old and had good teeth. In time, with good grass, it would fill out so nobody could count its ribs a hundred yards away.

Riding back to the painted canyon, he wondered if he'd done something dumb. Yep, he decided after thinking it over, it was dumb to alienate the town. He needed a town. Everyone needed a town now and then.

Sooner or later, and the sooner the better, he was going to have to go back and file a claim on the painted canyon.

He was bone weary, hungry, and half-asleep in the saddle when he got back. Her fire was a guiding light again. There was no show of emotion, no embrace when he dismounted before her. She used a shovel to smother the fire. Whether she liked it or not, he put an arm around her waist as he walked, leading the gray horse, into the canyon. There, he off-saddled and turned the horse in with the others, then went to the cave and all but collapsed on his bed.

While she watched, expressionless, he ate hot soup made of tiny bits of meat and diced potatoes, carrots and turnips. Tired as he was, he wished he could talk to her and tell her what had happened. She did understand the word, "Good," and his smile. She nodded and smiled back.

At the baby's cry, she went to it and cradled it in her lap.

Bill lay back on the bed and slept.

The gray horse earned its keep. Bill let it rest and crop the tall green grass a few days while he rode his other three saddle horses, then early one morning he saddled the gray. From sunup to sundown he rode, looking for his cattle, rounding up the ones he found and shoving them to the man-made pond. After four days, he calculated he had twenty-one cows and a bull still not located. He could only hope they hadn't been shot.

Fall was coming, and Bill knew he would soon have to build the cabin and fence for another horse pasture. He would also dig another dirt tank to catch and hold water.

As his dad had often said, "Growin' beef ain't all settin' on your ass in a saddle."

Too, he would have to go back to Colorado City, hunt up the land commissioner and file a homestead claim on a hundred and sixty acres surrounding the painted canyon. If he could find the sonofabitch. He'd take the wagon and buy some lumber while he was there. Try to, anyway. He grinned a wry grin and shook his head when he thought about it.

Going back to Colorado City wouldn't be a pleasure trip.

Using a lead pencil and a tablet of writing paper, he composed a message. While he wrote, he tried to recall the language in the few legal documents he had seen. He tore up the first sheet of paper, threw it into the cooking fire and tried again.

"To who it may concern," he wrote. That sheet also went into the fire. "To whom it may concern. I William C. Williams, claim a quarter section of land around a canyon, which I believe to be near the western boundary of El Paso County in Colorado Territory under the Homestead Act of..." He paused. When was that law passed? He continued... "1862. If this land is not avalable..." He used the eraser on the end of the pencil to rub out the last word. "...available, then I claim squatter's rights under the preemption laws."

Reading it over carefully, he added a comma after "Territory," and grinned to himself when he remembered Old Lady Hackett, the woman once hired to educate the Williams brothers. She would have thumped him on the head for leaving out a comma or misspelling a word. Bless her old soul, he said to himself. Wherever she is, I hope she's well and happy.

And I wish to hell she was here to write this letter.

That done, he looked around for the woman. He found her at the creek trying to brush off her one dress. She was stark naked. The dress was dirty and worn, and he realized it was the only garment she owned. Silently, he promised to buy her some clothes while he was in town. If he could. Meanwhile, the noon meal was cooking, the baby was asleep, and she was... Hell, he said to himself, why wait for night.

He was harnessing his Percherons at dawn and hitching them to the wagon. The woman had a stack of corncakes with fried bacon ready and wrapped in his rain slicker, and Bill had five double armloads of fresh cut grass piled in the wagon. He gathered the lines, climbed to the spring seat, and held up two fingers then three and pointed at the sky. She nodded to let him know she understood. As he drove away, the wagon wheels bouncing over the clump grass, he looked back and saw her watching him. She's afraid I'll leave some time and get killed and not come back, he said to himself.

And hell, who knows, she might be right.

He was on the wagon road eight or ten miles from town when he saw the buggy coming toward him. The man in the buggy was easy to recognize: blond curly hair, round, red, chubby face. Fat hands holding the lines.

When neighbors met they were supposed to stop and bat the breeze, talk about the weather, the grass, the cattle market, the coming winter. But this neighbor was no one that Bill wanted to visit with. He was an Easterner, and a mean sonofabitch who hired gunslingers to guarantee his conglomerate had all the free grass it wanted. One of those Eastern financiers. A money-grubber who would kill rather than lose on an investment.

It was kind of embarrassing to pass someone on a road without saying hello, or saying something, but that's what Bill did. One of the two had to get off the road to let the other pass, and Bill pulled his team to the right and looked straight ahead when the buggy went by.

As soon as he saw the town lights that night, he turned north to Owl Creek, and unhitched his team and pulled the harness off. After the horses drank their fill in the creek, he tied them to the wagon and let them eat the grass he'd cut. His supper was two of the corn cakes and two slices of cold bacon. He unrolled his bed near the wagon, pulled off his boots, crawled under the tarp and waited for daylight.

Almost everywhere he looked in Colorado City he could see buildings under construction. There were one-story houses for families and two-story wood-frame buildings for merchants. Good. With all the new people moving in, he would soon be a stranger and maybe he could start getting acquainted all over. But he wasn't a stranger yet. He was recognized.

"That's that Williams," a pedestrian said. "He's the one told us all to go to hell."

"Yup, that's him. Hear he's livin' with a squaw. Hear he's got a papoose."

"Say one thing fer 'im, he's got gall, comin' to town now."

Bill ignored them. And when he found himself on a collision course with another team and wagon, he "Whoaed" his team and let the other wagon pass. The driver recognized him too, gave him a startled look and then an angry scowl.

A steam whistle west of town summoned workers to a sawmill. Bill hoped the timberjacks and sawyers could keep up with the demand for building materials.

Someone ran and told Sheriff Ben Jenkins that Bill Williams was back in town, and the sheriff, his shaggy eyebrows pulled together, hurried to Colorado Street to watch him. Bill ignored him too. At the land commissioner's office, he tied his team to a stout hitching post and tried the door. Locked. Of course. When he turned to leave, a half-dozen men had gathered around, but made no move to bother him. Two boys, ten or twelve years old, sandy hair, baggy pants, came running up, stopped suddenly and stared.

Forcing a smile, Bill said, "Howdy kids."

They stared with mouths open. Then the shorter one uttered a tentative, "H-howdy. A-are you Bill Williams?"

"That's me. What's your name?"

"Uh, J-John. Are you the man that was in jail?"

"Yep. Are you the boy who talked to me through the window and told me how to find the Pritchards' place?"

"Y-yeah."

Still smiling, Bill said, "Well, maybe you would tell me where to find the county clerk. There is a county clerk, ain't there?"

"Uh, yeah. She's over at George's mercantile."

"What's her name?"

"Mrs. George."

"Thanks kid. Maybe I can return the favor some time." He untied the team, got back in the wagon and drove down the street until he came to a big sign telling the world that this was George's General Merchandise. It was a one-story log building with a false front, one of the oldest buildings on the street, and, Bill guessed, one of the oldest enterprises.

Again, he tied his team to a hitching post, and stepped up onto the plank walk. Sheriff Ben Jenkins was nearby, watching. Bill opened a plank door and went inside, removing his hat as he stepped across the threshold. A man with an eyeshade was counting a stack of overalls. A woman with an open ledger was writing down figures. They looked up, recognized him and frowned.

"Morning," Bill said, trying to be cheerful, "I'm looking for Mrs. George."

The woman's voice was icy, "I'm Mrs. George."

"Mrs. George, ma'am, I've been told that you are the county clerk."

"I am the duly elected clerk of El Paso County."

"Well, ma'am, I have to ask you a favor."

"Oh, you do."

The man said nothing, just listened.

Bill unbuttoned a shirt pocket and removed the folded letter he had carefully written. "Yes, ma'am. I've been trying to find the land

146

commissioner so I could file a homestead claim, and he's not to be found. What I need, ma'am, is someone I can trust, a public official like yourself, to hand him this letter."

"What does the letter say?"

"It says I'm laying claim to a hundred and sixty acres, like the law says I can, and it says where the land is. You'd be doing me a favor, ma'am, if you'd read it and remember what it says. In case it gets lost."

She unfolded the letter and read it carefully. The man read it too, over her shoulder. "And you want me to give this to Mr. Newton?"

"If you would, please. And I'd like for you to remember that you gave it to him."

She looked at the man. The man looked at her. She looked back at Bill. "It's my duty, I suppose, as an elected official."

Bill smiled. "I sure do thank you, Mrs. George." He turned to leave, saw several rolls of cloth, and stopped. "Uh, Mrs. George," he said, turning back, "I'd sure like to buy some of that cloth."

Still icy, "What do you want it for?"

"To make a dress. And I need some needles and thread."

Even colder, "For that savage woman?"

"Yes, ma'am."

"We don't sell to savages, do we, Amos." The man shook his head.

"I'll take care of this letter because it's my public duty, but we want no traffic with Indian lovers."

"Listen, Mrs. George," Bill was facing her, his hands hanging limp at his sides, "I've fought the Indians same as everybody and I've had some neighbors, good friends, killed by Indians. But I found a woman so sick she couldn't walk, and there was nobody else to take care of her so I took care of her."

She looked at the man. The man looked at her. She looked back at Bill. "You say she was sick?"

"Yes, ma'am. She was having a baby and she needed help. I'd have done the same for a wild animal."

"Well..." There was a long pause, and when she spoke again her voice wasn't so cold. "I'm a good Christian, and the Bible says to love thy neighbor. I'm going to ask Reverend Mosely about this."

"I sure would appreciate that, Mrs. George." He turned again to go.

"How much cloth do you want?"

Bill left the store feeling better about Colorado City. There was a church in town and Christian people. He wasn't a church-going man himself, but he liked people who were. Where there was a church and a school, justice would soon follow. As he climbed into the wagon, placing his package carefully under the seat, he was optimistic about the future.

Until he looked back and saw Sheriff Jenkins go into the store.

It wasn't hard to find a sawmill. All he had to do was head west out of town toward a column of smoke from a steam engine. When he got closer he heard the high-pitched whine of a power driven buzz saw and saw piles of pine logs and stacks of lumber. A man was using a cant hook to roll logs onto a wide belt which carried it to the saw, and another man was carrying lumber away from the saw to other men who stacked it in neat stacks. Two more men were using scoop shovels to shovel sawdust into a wagon.

Bill turned his team toward a one-room shack which he reckoned was the office. It was empty, but it held a desk littered with papers. "Want something, mister?" A short, husky man with a wad of tobacco bulging one cheek, came out of a nearby toilet buttoning the suspenders of his overalls.

"Yeah, I need some one-inch boards."

"Top grade?"

"No, it doesn't have to be top grade."

"How much?"

"All I can put in that wagon."

"Suddenly, the man squinted at Bill, spat a stream of tobacco juice at a rock and squinted again. "Say, ain't you...?"

"Yeah," Bill stood with his hands on his hips and looked the man squarely in the face, "I'm Bill Williams. I'm the one that broke out of jail and told the town to go to hell, and I'm the one that's living with a squaw."

148

Turning his head, the man squirted another stream of tobacco juice onto the dry ground. "We ain't got no lumber for sale right now."

"What do you mean? It's piled all over the place."

"It's sold. They're buyin' it faster'n we can cut it."

"You mean you don't want to sell to me." It was a statement, not a question.

The man looked at the six-gun on Bill's right hip, hanging low, and he looked at the hard lines of Bill's face. Turning his head again he unleashed another brown stream and yelled at two men stacking lumber, "Hey, c'mere."

"You won't need any help," Bill said, "I ain't gonna try to rob you."

The two men came over, question marks on their faces. Both were unarmed.

"Get them rifles out of the office, this here gent's a troublemaker."

"I told you I won't cause any trouble," Bill said. "And I'll tell you something else, you can go to hell too." He went to his wagon, climbed up to the seat, and without looking at the men, clucked to his team. The wagon rattled away.

Another sawmill sent up another column of smoke about a mile south, and Bill headed in that direction. There, he was recognized immediately, but the businessman in a wrinkled suit and dark red necktie offered to sell him some lumber.

"Four cents a board foot."

"Ain't that a little steep?"

"Not for you, mister. I know who you are. And I can sell all the lumber I've got for any price I want."

Bill uttered one word: "Shit."

On his way back to town, he swore to himself, "So there's some good Christians in town. Hell, in every town there has to be some mean sonsofbitches too. Goddamn merchants. The town is growing and they're jacking up their prices and getting rich. No wonder every merchant in the country wants the population to grow. Goddamn."

He was so angry he paid no attention to the heavy traffic when he plow-lined his team onto Colorado Street. The street was crowded with freight wagons, buggies, horsebackers and pedestrians. He paid no attention to the heavy freight wagon coming toward him, pulled by a four-horse team.

He felt the bump when a rear hub on his light wagon collided with a rear hub on the freight wagon. He felt an even bigger bump when his wheel came off and the right rear corner of his wagon dropped to the ground.

His Percherons felt it too, didn't like what was happening and bolted. For the next ten seconds they dragged the wagon down the street with one axle plowing a furrow. Bill was busy hauling on the lines and saying "Whoa" in a quiet, soothing voice. Someone shouted "Runaway, runaway." Pedestrians scattered off the street. Other teamsters, trying to head off another wreck, were whoaing their horses.

"Ho-o-o," Bill said, sawing on the lines. "Ho-o-o, now."

Finally, the Percherons slowed and stopped, nervous, stamping their feet, pulling on the bits. Bill couldn't get down from his wagon without slacking up on the lines. All he could do was keep his seat and look back. His right rear axle was dragging and his wheel was lying in the street a hundred yards behind him. The teamster of the freight wagon had stopped his team and was looking back, but he too had to keep his seat and hang onto the lines.

Two men hurried up and grabbed the bridles on Bill's horses, allowing him to climb down.

"They ain't used to all this fuss and racket," Bill said.

"It could of been a bad one, mister. We could of had horses down and harness and wagons tangled up all over the street."

"Yeah, it's probably my fault. I should've taken a street that wasn't so crowded."

"Say, ain't you...?"

"Yeah, that's me."

Both men immediately let go of the bridles, but the horses were quiet now. Bill held onto the lines as he climbed back to the seat.

CHAPTER 23

For a moment, he didn't know what to do. He couldn't let go of his horses and go back and pick up the wheel, and he couldn't unhitch the horses right there on the main street. There was only one thing to do, he decided finally. He clucked to the team and they jerked forward, then slowed to a walk at Bill's urging, dragging the wagon. Dragged it until the axle bent and kept on dragging it. At the first intersection, Bill pulled them to the right and went down a side street to an alley. In the alley he stopped, got down, unhitched the horses, and tied them to the wagon.

It was a relief to see the axle wasn't broken. Only the end, the iron part, was bent. That could be taken off, heated, pounded straight, and put back on. First, he'd have to get the wheel.

People stared, but nobody moved his way as he picked up the wheel and rolled it down the street and around the corner to his wagon. Again, he was relieved to see the wheel wasn't damaged. But the fist-sized nut that held the wheel on the axle had come off, and he had to go back on the street and look for it.

He heard them talking while he looked for the nut. "That's that Williams," a woman said. "You know, the Indian lover. He lives with a squaw and he's got a papoose."

"What's he looking for?"

"A wheel came off his wagon and he's looking for the pieces."

"Well, ain't nobody here gonna help 'im. Not him."

Once he found the nut, Bill had to take the iron end off the axle.

151

It fit onto the wooden axle like a sleeve and was bolted on. Luckily, he'd always carried a monkey wrench, a hammer and some nails in a tool box under the wagon seat, and he got the iron end off with no trouble. Then, carrying it, he went looking for a blacksmith shop.

"Say, ain't you..." The blacksmith was squatting under a horse, holding the horse's left hind leg across his thigh. He had a full beard, black, and his face was grimy with smoke and sweat. A few horseshoe nails stuck out of one corner of his mouth. He let the horse's foot down, straightened and took the nails out of his mouth. He was bare chested and big, about two axe handles across the shoulders. All muscle.

"Yeah," Bill sighed with resignation. He was getting damned tired of this, but he was tired of arguing with everybody too.

"What is it you said you want?"

Showing him the bent iron, Bill explained that it had to be straightened.

"Can't get to it now. You'll have to wait."

"Won't take but a minute or two."

"Take longer'n that. I'll have to stoke up the fire and I ain't got time now. See those two horses yonder." He pointed his shoeing hammer at two saddle horses tied to a hitch rail. "Gotta be shod. Belong to some folks goin' up in the high hills."

"Maybe it won't have to be heated. If I can use your anvil and a heavy hammer I might be able to straighten it myself."

"Huh-uh. Nobody uses my tools but me."

"All right, how long will I have to wait?"

"Soon's I get me some dinner I'll finish shoeing this horse and then I'll shoe them two and then if I ain't got nothin' else to do I'll see if I can straighten that iron you got."

"Listen, you'll have to heat those horseshoes and you might as well put this in the fire too. When it gets hot enough it won't take but a minute to pound it straight. And I can be on my way."

"No."

"Why?"

The blacksmith's upper arms were almost as big as Bill's thighs, and he made certain Bill noticed it. "'Cause I don't want to, and if that ain't reason enough I'll think of another'n."

152

Bill's first impulse was to say something insulting, but that would be useless. He had to get the iron straightened, and he couldn't straighten it by pounding it on a rock with the light hammer he had. Later in the day was better than no time at all. Besides, if he got in a fight with this hulk he'd have to use a gun or get the stuffing beat out of him. "All right," he said, "I'll be back later." The blacksmith paid him no attention as he walked away.

"What the hell else is going to go wrong?" Bill muttered. "Not one damn thing has gone right. Dammit, I'd be better off going to Pueblo or even Denver."

His meal was another corncake and another slice of bacon. No use inviting a fight by going to a cafe. After he ate, he led his horses to an irrigation ditch that crossed a vacant lot and let them drink. He let them crop the grass in the lot too, and half-expected someone to come along and accuse him of trespassing. At three o'clock by the sun he went back to the blacksmith shop. The smith was shaping an iron rim for a wagon wheel.

"Not yet."

Bill sat on the ground under a tree and leaned back against the tree, wondering if he was wasting his time. That big pile of manure was making him wait out of meanness and nothing else. Hell, he might let him wait and still refuse to straighten the axle iron. What would he do if that happened? He'd be fighting mad. He couldn't allow anyone to treat him that way, no matter how big.

The longer he waited the angrier he got. In his mind he could picture the smith bragging in one of the saloons about how he made that Injun lover wait most of the day and then left him with his mouth hanging open. Wouldn't they get a laugh out of that. Yeah, they'd think that was a great joke. Lots of fun.

Near sundown when the smith put out his forge fire and started gathering his tools, Bill jumped up. Without a word, he went inside the shop, grabbed the biggest hammer he saw, put his axle iron on an anvil and pounded.

"Hey, what the hell you think you're doin'?"

Jaws clamped shut, Bill pounded, turned the iron and pounded the other side. Big hands suddenly had him by the shoulders, spinning him around. A big fist came from somewhere. But Bill was expecting it, and jumped sideways, letting the fist go past his face. He skipped away from the smith, then held the hammer up between them.

"Stop right there." He barked the words. His voice was menacing. "Take one more step and I'll lay this hammer upside your head."

The smith stopped, big fists balled and ready to strike.

"I'm gonna straighten this iron and then I'll go. If you try to stop me I'm gonna tear your goddamn head off and poke it up your dying ass. If you don't think so, just try me."

He meant it, and his face and voice showed it. Not only that, this was the man who'd busted out of jail and told the sheriff and the whole town to go to hell. And if he was fighting mad then, he was killing mad now. The smith stood still.

Keeping the anvil between him and the bearded hulk, Bill pounded the iron. It would have been a simple job if he could have heated it, and having to keep one eye on the hulk made it even more difficult. But slowly it was being straightened. When it was almost, but not quite, straight, Bill quit. It would have to do. The wheel would wobble, but when he got back to the painted canyon he could heat the iron enough to do the job right.

He backed away, holding the iron in one hand and the hammer in the other. The smith still hadn't moved. Finally, he threw the hammer in the direction of the forge, turned and sauntered back to his wagon.

He had it figured out. The smith had planned to do some bragging about the way he put that squawman in his place, but now he had nothing to brag about. Now he'd have to tell another story. If he told about it at all.

He wouldn't tell.

The next job was easier. A piece of a building block lay in the alley not far from the wagon, and Bill carried it over and put it down next to the end of the rear axle. He straddled the axle, bent his knees, took hold and, grunting and straining, raised the axle enough that he could kick one end of the block under it. Now he had it off the ground and could slip the sleeve of the axle iron into place and bolt it there.

That done, he straightened up and realized he had another problem.

There was no way one man could raise that axle high enough to put the wheel on it. If he had a long pole, he could turn the piece of building block on end, use it for a fulcrum and pry the rear of the wagon up. But he couldn't hold the pole down and put the wheel on too. Besides, he didn't have a long pole. He had to have help.

Help? Where the hell was he going to get help? Not in Colorado City. Folks here wouldn't give him a drink of water. They hated Indians and they hated Indian lovers. He'd be treated like a beggar if he asked for help in Colorado City.

But wait a minute. All those saloons didn't cater just to the local people. What kept so many saloons in business were the sourdoughs who came down from the hills with gold dust and nuggets in their pockets. And the freighters going through town. And the cowboys from out of town. If he approached the right men, he might get some help after all. How to go about it?

There was only one way. Bill saw that his team was resting, tied to the wagon with the harness on, then went back to Colorado Street. Dark was coming on and he didn't have too much time. It would be doubly hard to put a wheel on in the dark. Wagon traffic had thinned out now, but there was more horseback traffic, and more horses were tied to the hitchracks on the street. On the plank walk, he *thump-thumped* his way past a saloon. It held customers, but not so many that the bartender didn't have time to visit with them. Two doors down, he came to another saloon. This one was crowded. The bartender here was working as fast as he could with both hands. He didn't even have time to look up. This one was as good as any.

He started to step through the open door and stopped when, out of the corner of his eye, he saw two riders coming down the street. They looked familiar. It only took another glance to recognize them. Gar and the other Ladder tough. Their horses were tired, looked as if they'd come too far too fast. The riders were tired too, slouching in their saddles. Gar recognized Bill, reined up, scowled, then as if changing his mind, went on down the street.

At first Bill recognized no one in the saloon. There were all kinds of men, from well-dressed merchants in finger-length coats, fancy vests and cravats at their throats, to the sourdoughs in baggy pants and jackboots. There were a few cowboys too, who, like Bill never took their spurs off their boots. Four men were pounding the pinewood bar with their fists and clamoring for the harried bartender to pour faster. "Hey, barkeep, hurry ever' chance you get," yelled a cowboy with a grin.

"Ah'm so dry Ah'm spittin' wind," said another, also grinning. Bill recognized that one. It was the tall thin galoot with the bobbing adams apple who worked for the Ladder.

With Ladder men present, this wasn't the place to look for help, and Bill decided to go. But the thin galoot recognized him, and hollered, "Hey. Hey, uh, Texas. Hold up a minute." He stomped over. His face with its sad drooping eyes was serious but not threatening.

"Yeah?" Bill faced him, afraid he was in for a fight and not wanting to fight.

"Ah wanta buy you a drink of whiskey," the thin galoot said. "Ah owe you a drink."

Bill couldn't believe it. "You want to buy me a drink?"

"Yeah, now listen here, don't go grabbin' your iron or anything 'til Ah s'plain somethin'."

Bill's eyes went over the crowd. No one was paying any attention to him. "What?"

"You might not know it, but Ah saved your life. Shore, Ah he'ped git you locked up in jail, but that was better'n bein' shot down right whar you stood. Wasn't it?"

Thinking it over, Bill remembered that this man was the first to notice he was riding another man's horse out there near the painted canyon and suggested he be taken to town instead of shot.

"In a way, I reckon you did save my bacon. Why?"

"Like Ah said, Ah'm from Texas too, and..." Tex glanced around with a furtive look in his eye, "Ah don't cotton much to some a the stuff that goes on at the Ladder outfit. Matter of fact, Ah done rolled up my bed this mornin. Ah'm headin' back south."

"What kind of stuff goes on?"

"Ah ain't spillin' the beans. But Ah'm headin' out. First, howsomever, Ah'd admire to have a drink with you just to show you Ah ain't got no hard feelin's. Hell, we might run onto one another agin, somewhars."

156

Bill didn't want to drink with him. So his conscience was bothering him. There was no excuse for ever working for an outfit like the Ladder. "I didn't come here to drink. I'm looking for help putting a wheel back on my wagon."

"Ah'll he'p you. Whar is your wagon?"

"In an alley down the street, but it'll take more than two men. Three at least, and we ought to have four. Three to raise the corner of the wagon and another to put the wheel on."

"W-e-e-l, the onliest man I know in here works for the Ladder. But tell you what, let's have us a drink of whiskey and purty soon we'll find somebody."

Bill had known, when he came into the saloon, he'd have to order a drink before he could get into a conversation and find some help, but still he was reluctant to drink with this man. "Listen, if we ever meet again I won't start a fight or even say anything about you, but I don't think we'll ever be pals."

The thin galoot's sad eyes grew sadder. Then suddenly they widened. "Oh-oh," he said, his voice low, "you're gonna need all the friends you can git. Look who just come in."

Bill looked behind him. Gar and the other Ladder tough were standing in the open door. They stood spraddle legged with their hands on their hips close to their guns.

CHAPTER 24

The two gunmen stood shoulder to shoulder in the door where nobody could get in or out. Bill could tell by their faces they weren't about to let him out. He glanced around. The saloon was nearly full of men haw-hawing, yelling across the room at each other and gulping whiskey as fast as the bartender could pour it. The two toughs hadn't been noticed—yet. He had no chance in a gunfight. His six-gun was holstered on his right side where he could draw it faster, but he knew he couldn't outdraw and outshoot two professional gunhands. Maybe, if he was lucky, mighty lucky, he could get one, but the other would get him.

Run? That would be the smart thing to do. Where? Into the milling mob of boozers. Get in among them where they couldn't shoot without hitting someone they didn't want to hit. Then work his way to the back door. There had to be a back door. Run, Bill Williams.

It was a familiar feeling. His feet wanted to run, but his mind didn't.

What, then?

Gar and his partner didn't move, just stood there and dared Bill to move. What if he didn't move? Let them make the first move. See what they had in mind to do. Bill stood the same way they did, hands on hips, feet apart, and stared right back at them. He felt, rather than saw, the galoot called Tex slip away behind him. Slip away and fade into the crowd. Tex didn't want to tangle with these two. The haw-hawing continued. Finally a man in ragged clothes and jackboots tried to get through the door. When he saw the door blocked, he halted, scratched his scraggly beard, then tried to push his way out. He was shoved roughly backward. His hand went to his gun. Stopped. He knew now what he was facing. He too backed into the mob.

Gar spoke. His voice was deadly. "What the hell you doin' in here with white folks, Williams?" Then louder, "Squawman Williams, I ask you somethin'."

The mob quieted. Someone said, "Is that that Williams?" No one answered.

Gar repeated, "I ask you a question, Williams. Injun lover. Squaw humper."

Bill fixed his gaze on the bridge of Gar's nose. He tried to keep his heart from pounding. He tried to put some bravado in his voice. "You were gonna whip me with your fists once, Gar, but you weren't man enough to do it. You had to have some help. If you're so goddamn tough why don't you try it again." In a fist fight he had a chance. In a gunfight he didn't.

"I'll whup you, all right. I'm gonna put a .44 slug right up your Injun-lovin' ass."

"Yeah." The other tough spoke for the first time. "We kicked the shit out of the Cheyennes and run 'em all out of the country, all 'cept one, and that's the one you're shackin' up with."

There was nothing Bill could say to that. This was no place to try to explain why he was living with a squaw.

Men behind him began moving aside, slowly, trying not to be obvious about it, but wanting to get out of the line of fire. None of them spoke, just listened and watched.

Bill reckoned Gar would be the first to grab for his gun. He watched Gar's eyes, hoping they would give him a split-second warning. Still, no one moved. Come on, Bill's mind said. Come on, let's get this over with.

Then on second thought, keep talking. Maybe a miracle would happen.

"How much are they paying you? You know who I mean. The conglomerate. Those Eastern and Dutch money grubbers. That scheming Aarnstadt."

"Just keep jawin', Injun lover, and I'll put the first slug in your gut and let you die lookin' at your innards."

No miracle was going to happen. The shooting was about to start. Why wait. Move first. No. That's what they want. They want to tell the world that he reached for his gun first and they were only defending themselves. They watched his eyes. He watched Gar's. His mind was racing. He ordered it to slow down, to think. All right, if he was going to die, everybody in the saloon and then everybody in Colorado City was going to know he was murdered by hired gunmen. Maybe they would be hung for it. Maybe.

Bill let his hands drop to his sides away from his gun. He took a step toward Gar. Another step. "I'm leaving," he said. "Kindly step aside."

Gar barely moved his mouth when he spoke again, "You're not walkin' out, Squawman. You're goin' out feet first."

He was close enough to smell Gar's breath. Close enough to reach him.

Moving as fast as he could and with all the strength he had, Bill brought a hard fist up from his knees, aimed at Gar's jaw.

It took only a small fraction of a second for the blow to land, but in that instant Gar managed to get his six-gun half out of its holster.

Only half-out.

Gar's head snapped back, his eyes crossed and his knees went weak. But there was that other gunman. His gun was clear and the hammer was back.

Bill spun to his left, away from the man's right hand. He heard the ear-splitting boom as the gun went off, and he backed into the man. Slammed into him. Slammed him so hard the second shot was spoiled too. Bill brought his left elbow up fast and hit the gunman a staggering blow in the face. With his right hand he drew his own .44, thumbed the hammer back, shoved the bore into the man's stomach and fired.

The sound was muffled, but not the impact. Gar's partner dropped like a wet dishrag.

The fight wasn't over. Gar had recovered his balance and had the gun in his hand. He'd done something that took a lot of practice, drawing his gun and cocking the hammer back in the same split second. Bill didn't have time to cock his gun. Didn't have time to shoot again. Instead, he swung the gun barrel at Gar's head. It connected at the same time Gar's six-gun boomed.

He thought he'd been hit. His right side went numb. The slug had hit something, some part of him. Gritting his teeth he swung the gun barrel again. Swung it and swung it. Gar went down, stayed down.

Bill kicked the gun out of Gar's hand. Kicked it again and sent it skittering across the wooden floor. He stood there, feeling dizzy and wondering why he was alive.

No one moved. No one spoke. Bill Williams couldn't believe it. The two professional gunslingers were down and he was still standing. He looked at himself, expecting to see blood. His wound had to be the kind that wouldn't be felt until later when the shock more off. Men had been shot without knowing it until later. Shot fatally. Why was there no blood?

He moved, and his right hip felt stiff, awkward. Looking again, he saw why. The gun holster was out of place, around behind him. A bullet had punched a neat hole through it, front to back. It was the holster that had been hit.

A sigh came out of him, and he looked at the crowd. Still, no one moved. With awkward fingers, he turned the cartridge belt until the holster was in place on his right hip. He let the hammer down on his six-gun, holstered it, then spun on his heels and walked with wooden steps out of the building.

Night had come on. A hunchbacked man was using a long pole to raise a lighted lantern to the top of a tall post on the corner. The cool night air felt good. Bill breathed deeply, filling his lungs. Until now he'd been feeling numb as if he'd been yanked from the jaws of death and couldn't believe it. But the night air brought him back to his senses, and he heard loud voices behind him. Excited voices.

No telling what the mob in the saloon would do. They might come after him or they might get the sheriff. They sure would get the sheriff, and Sheriff Jenkins was looking for an excuse to hang him. Move, Bill Williams, he told himself. He ran, boots thumping on the boardwalk, to the corner, around the corner and down the alley. He ran to his wagon and horses. There, he stopped and listened. No sound of pursuit. They were going for Ben Jenkins, intending to let him do the pursuing. They would help, but they wanted an official leader.

Fingers moving as fast as he could make them move, he stripped the harness off the Percherons, pulled the bridle off one, cut the lines to make two short reins for the other and scrambled onto the big horse's back. He would have to leave one horse, his wagon and everything. No, not everything. Leaning low, he reached into the wagon and grabbed his Winchester and the paper-wrapped roll of cloth. Then he touched spurs to the big horse's sides and said, "Come on, old pony, let's lope."

The Percheron's running gait was heavy-footed and awkward but it pounded down the alley, across a street, down another alley and on out of town. Bill kept the big horse running for about three miles, until it began weakening, then stopped. Its sides were heaving and its nostrils blowing, and Bill apologized. "You're not made for this kind of work, old feller, but you're all I've got right now."

It was dark enough that any pursuers wouldn't be able to see him, and he rode on, letting the horse walk until it got its wind. At the same time he listened, hoping he could hear any riders that might be coming his way. He heard nothing.

Could it be there was no pursuit? He stopped his horse still and listened carefully. That stump-headed sheriff would want to jail him and hang him. Why wasn't he coming after him with a dozen deputized men? Maybe...maybe they figured they couldn't find him in the dark and they were waiting for daylight. They knew where he was heading. Sure, they knew. Some of the Ladder riders had seen the painted canyon and they knew he'd be going back there. No, that didn't make sense either. If they waited for daylight, he could be on a fresh horse and halfway to Texas before they found the place.

Another possibility came to Bill's mind. A mob of men saw what happened in the saloon, and could tell the sheriff how Bill had fought in self-defense. The two toughs had drawn their guns first. As hard as it was to believe, it was true. Still, he had killed one man and knocked the hell out of another and the sheriff couldn't let him just ride away. There had to be an inquest of some kind.

Damned strange.

All right, here's their plan. They figure he won't head back to

Texas. He's got cattle, horses and tools and he won't leave all that and run. He'll be there when they want him. And maybe Ben Jenkins can turn the truth around and make it sound like he killed a man and pistol whipped another just because they worked for the Ladder.

Aw, dammit, there were too many witnesses. Too many maybes.

And here's another: the sheriff hopes he won't give up without a fight and he'll be killed. That would be the end of Bill Williams, and no questions asked. That's what the conglomerate wants, and Ben Jenkins takes payoffs from the conglomerate. They don't want him arrested, they want him dead.

That gave him three choices: he could fight and see how many he could kill before they killed him. He could run. Or he could surrender peacefully and depend on witnesses to clear him of any crime. When he thought about it, he really had no choice. He didn't want to kill any more men and he sure didn't want to be killed. Running would make him an outlaw, always looking over his shoulder. Giving up without a fight was no guarantee of anything, but it was his best shot. At least it would give him a chance to turn his horses out, find his other Percheron, put the wheel back on his wagon, and try to live peacefully. Yeah, that's what he'd do.

He rode on in the dark, knowing he was heading in the right direction, but knowing he'd never find the painted canyon without the woman's guiding light.

It was around midnight, by his calculations, when he began looking for the fire. He should be able to see it now, away off in the distance. The big horse's back dipped as it dropped into the draws and swerved as it skirted the deep gulches. Bill wished the horse had been kept at the painted canyon long enough to know the place as home. If it had, it would go there. The horse could find it in the dark. Why was there no fire?

Did the woman finally decide to leave and hunt for her people?

Two hours later, he stopped and slid down. A man could wander around here all night. Nobody but an animal—or an Indian—could find that canyon in the dark. It might be five hundred yards away or it might be five miles away. Without the woman's fire, he'd have to wait for daylight.

Hanging onto the short reins, Bill sat on the ground and hugged his knees. The Winchester and the paper-wrapped bundle lay on the ground beside him. The horse wanted to graze, but the reins were too short and Bill had to hang onto the reins. Finally, the animal gave up and stood with its head down and its nose only a few inches from Bill's hat. Both man and horse dozed.

As soon as he could see anything at all, he scrambled onto the big horse's back, hanging onto his package and the Winchester. His gurgling stomach reminded him he needed food and his parched throat reminded him he needed water. The horse was happy to be moving again. They went on, and soon Bill realized he was too far east. He plowlined the Percheron back west, and within an hour knew where he was. It took only another half hour to come to his dirt tank and the diversion ditch.

But where was the woman?

Sadly, Bill concluded, as he slid off the big horse's back and opened the wire gate at the mouth of the canyon, that she had gone. He'd expected it. She was homesick for her people, and by showing Bill the painted canyon and a good place to homestead, she had paid her debt to him.

His saddle horses were there and well-fed from the tall grass. His saddle lay on a spot of bare ground, covered with the saddle blanket. She had left walking, no doubt carrying her baby in a sling on her back and carrying some of the antelope meat. "Here's hoping you find your people, Little Mouse," he said to himself. "Here's hoping you and your baby live a good life."

It wasn't until he walked into the cave that he saw their bodies.

164

CHAPTER 25

The baby lay crumpled against a wall, its head a bloody mess. A spot of blood on the wall told him what happened. Someone had grabbed the baby by the feet and swung it against the wall.

The woman was naked, on her back with her legs apart, the same position she was in the first time he saw her. Only now her dark eyes were staring sightlessly at the ceiling. A small round hole in her left breast was ringed with dried blood.

She had been shot. Shot and raped.

Bill Williams let out a long painful groan and dropped to his knees beside her. He touched her hand. Her skin was cold, the fingers stiff. He groaned again and put his face in his hands.

In a muffled voice, he mumbled, "My God, Little Mouse. Oh my God."

For a long time he sat there, forgetting about hunger and a parched throat. He sat there until his limbs were stiff and aching. Finally, he stood and walked out of the cave, down the stone steps, feeling terribly weary, as if the world had dealt him a blow he couldn't bear.

Without knowing where he was going, he walked out of the canyon and stood on the rim, near the dirt tank. His eyes saw nothing. He stood there for a long time, then moving with wooden steps he went back and picked up a shovel.

It took two hours to dig a hole long enough, wide enough and deep enough. It had to be so deep that the coyotes wouldn't smell the bodies and dig them up. Then, back in the cave, he laid her on the buffalo robe, put the baby on top of her and crossed her arms over its body. Her arms were stiff and hard to move, but he managed to move them.

In spite of his weariness, the bodies weren't heavy. She was just a little bit of a thing. He carried them wrapped in the buffalo robe to the top of the rim. Let's see, he'd heard somewhere that Indians liked to be buried facing the sunrise. He didn't know whether that was true, but that's the way he laid them.

A short piece of board, part of the remains of his tarpaper shack on Owl Creek, served as a head board. He carved her name—the only name he knew her by—on the board. LITTLE MOUSE AND SON. He nailed the board to a post and drove the post into the ground at the head of the grave.

Still moving wearily, he went back to the cave and rummaged through a pack pannier until he found his tablet of paper and lead pencil. The pencil had to be sharpened with his pocket knife. Then he wrote a long letter to his brothers. He told them everything that had happened since leaving Wyoming, about the Cheyenne, the conglomerate and the Ladder, the Indian woman and her baby, the painted canyon, the treatment he got from the merchants in Colorado City. He told them where they could find the Running W cattle and horses, everything. Four times he had to stop and rest his writing hand. He concluded with:

"I don't know when I will see you again. You know I cannot let this pass. I will have to do something, and whatever I do will put me on the wrong side of the law. My hope is that it will all be forgotten some day and I can go back home. That is my biggest wish. Until then, God bless you both. Your brother, William."

Carefully, he folded the letter, put it in an envelope, sealed the envelope and wrote his brothers' address on it. He didn't know when or where he would post it, but sometime, some place within the next week or so.

A gnawing in the pit of his stomach reminded him he was hungry. He didn't want to eat. He had to eat. The meat the woman had cooked was still sitting in the dead ashes of her cooking fire. He couldn't eat it. The killers might have touched it. Outside, on a flat rock, she had placed strips of antelope meat to dry in the sun. It was as tough as leather, but he knew from experience that it was nourishment. It could be soaked and then eaten, used in a stew, or cut off a small piece at a time and held in his mouth until it softened. This time he dropped pieces in water with every kind of vegetable he had. He needed a strong meal.

While it was cooking, he loaded his pack panniers with everything but the soup pot and a spoon. They would have to go last. He rolled up his bed and tied it with two old broken bridle reins. Glad now that he hadn't pulled the shoes off his horses, he checked the feet of the long-legged sorrel and the dun. The shoes wouldn't have to be reset for a few more weeks. Using a pair of nippers, he clipped the nails and pried the shoes off the other horses, then opened the wire gate and let them out. No telling when they'd see another human being. "Drift south," he told them. "Winter's coming."

He ate. Forced himself to eat. The stew would have tasted better if he'd allowed it to cook longer and slower, but he got it down. Not much left to do after that. The two guns, the six-shooter and the Winchester, were in good condition and loaded. The keg of black blasting powder he'd bought long ago—what seemed like long ago—was still half-full.

Everything was ready. All he could do now was wait. Not for daylight this time. Wait for darkness. It was easy to figure out what had happened.

Someone from the Ladder had seen him drive his team and wagon into town. Gar and the other Ladder gunslinger were sent here while he was gone to kill the Indian woman and her baby. Rape her if they wanted, but kill her. He had seen them ride into Colorado City late yesterday on tired horses. They had done what they were told to do by the Dutchman, old Aarnstadt. Bill would have bet anything that someone from the Ladder had filed a homestead claim yesterday on the painted canyon. That claim would be dated earlier than his. The work he had done, the dirt tank he had built, would now be Ladder property.

And it was easy to figure out why they didn't chase after him last night and why they didn't come for him today. The sheriff was talked out of it. "Huh," Bill snorted out loud when he thought about it. Old Aarnstadt and the Ladder gunsels knew what was here. They sure didn't want the townsmen coming here and finding the bodies with limbs stiff from rigor mortis. That would be proof that they had been murdered yesterday when Bill Williams was in town. The townsmen would get suspicious.

And it would serve no purpose for Bill to go back to town and report the murders. No one would care. The Indian woman and her baby were savages. Not even human.

Shaking his head sadly, Bill allowed, "Maybe they're not to blame. I don't know. I don't know who's right and who's wrong. I'm betting there will always be a disagreement on that."

But he did know what he had to do.

Night was coming. It was time to go. He put his saddle on the sorrel and the crossbuck saddle on the dun. The canvas panniers were already loaded, each weighing approximately the same, and he hung them over the crossbucks, one on each side of the horse. His bedroll went on top of them and the powder keg on top of that. A box hitch held it all down. The Winchester was in the saddle boot and the six-gun was in his belt holster.

His tools, the remainder of his building materials, all were left behind.

Also left behind was a paper-wrapped package of dress material.

He picked up the packhorse's lead rope and mounted. It was turning dark as he rode out of the canyon. His other horses were grazing nearby, not yet aware that they were free. At the grave, he paused a moment, and removed his hat.

"Goodby, Little Mouse."

He rode at a slow walk, letting the horses take it easy. They'd have their work cut out for them later. He rode over the Colorado plains, across the draws and gulches, through the wheat grass, buffalo and gramma grass, around the yucca. Soapweeds, most folks called them. He knew where he was going, but again he needed lights to show him the place.

About ten o'clock by his calculation he rode up a long, low rise and saw the lights. There, he dismounted, but held onto the sorrel's reins. The ranch buildings were grouped along a creek, Owl Creek, where water was plentiful and the cottonwoods provided shade in the summer. Dim lamp lights showed in the windows of two of the buildings: the bunkhouse where the hired men unrolled their beds and the main house where old Aarnstadt lived. No curtains on the windows. No women on the Ladder.

With loosened cinches, the horses rested better. Bill took the keg of black powder off the pack horse and pulled out the stopper. Squatting, he watched the buildings and figured out a plan of action. He had to plan it well. Couldn't overlook anything. How many horses were in the corrals? Was there a fence between him and the buildings? Was there a back door to the main house? Where would he position himself?

Watching and waiting, he felt calm and cool. Why was he so calm? Just how did he feel? He tried to understand. It was anger, that was for sure. They had schemed, cheated, bribed public officials, tried to kill him and blame it on the Cheyenne, beat him up, turned the whole town against him, shot some of his cattle, then murdered the woman and her baby. Sure, he was angry. But there was more.

Revenge? Yeah, he admitted to himself, there was that. Nothing wrong with revenge. But there was still more. Duty?

If justice was to come to the West, men like that couldn't be allowed to go unpunished. The law was weak and the sheriff was corrupt. When the law didn't do its job, someone else had to.

Sitting there, watching the ranch buildings, Bill didn't consider himself a vigilante. That was the last thing he wanted to be. He'd seen a man hung once, and though he couldn't blame the men who did the hanging, he'd felt sorry for the poor devil.

The lights went out in the main house first, then in the bunkhouse. Bill stood and tightened the cinches on the saddles.

Someone had to do it.

He walked, leading the horses and carrying the keg of powder under his left arm. He led them down the hill to a corral, surprised to find no fence for a horse pasture. Probably on the other side of the corrals. He tied the pack horse to the saddle horn on the sorrel and tied the sorrel to a corral post. The night was black, but a quarter moon showed him a dim outline of the roofs, the corral posts and a three-sided stock shelter. He heard a horse snort.

Sure, there had to be at least one horse. A night horse, used to wrangle in the remuda in the morning. Groping his way, Bill found a gate. He unlatched it and swung it open, slowly, carefully, hoping the hinges wouldn't squeak. The horse trotted out, stopped and whinnied, trying to locate the remuda.

Uh-oh, Bill said under his breath. Someone could get suspicious. Squatting in the dark, he watched the bunkhouse, expecting to see the door open with a light behind it. Hoofbeats and a moving dark shape told him there was another horse in an adjacent corral. He watched the houses. Watched them for ten minutes.

Working by feel, he crawled through corral poles and found another gate, opened it. The horse almost knocked him down as it ran out, happy to be free. That did it, he thought. They'd hear the hoofbeats and come running.

Moving faster now, he went to his horses and lifted the Winchester out of the saddle boot. He'd get one or two of them. That wasn't what he'd planned, but that was better than nothing.

Waited. Watched.

They must be sound sleepers. He tried to remember what the ranch buildings were built of. He'd seen them only once before and that was from a distance. Lumber, he remembered. Rough and thick. One-and-a-half-inch planks with batten, probably. Maybe the walls were thick enough that the sound of hoofbeats didn't penetrate.

All right, they're not coming, and they're afoot. It will take some doing to catch those horses on foot, and it would be impossible in the dark. It's a long walk to town.

Now Bill crawled back through the corral poles, carrying his rifle and the powder keg. He groped his way across two corrals, and found himself next to a cattle chute made of two-inch planks. It wouldn't stop a .44 slug, but it was a better fortress than nothing. He left his rifle there, propped against the chute, not sure that that was the smart thing to do, and crept on foot to the bunkhouse. He might need the rifle, but he also needed two hands to do what he had to do. At the door to the bunkhouse, he stopped and listened. Uh-oh. The floorboards creaked. Someone was moving inside.

Bill moved too. Back around the corner of the building. Got there just as the door opened.

A man stood in the door. Stood there a long moment. Someone inside the bunkhouse said, "'Smatter, Gar?"

"I dunno. Keep thinkin' I hear somethin'."

"You worried about that squawman?"

"Naw. He's been a lucky sonofabitch, but his luck can't last."

"Why you hangin' on to that scattergun, then?"

"'Cause I feel better with a gun in my hands, that's why."

"Shit. You're worried."

"Naw. I just keep hearin' somethin', that's all."

"It's that stud horse. He's always runnin' around in his pen and raisin' a fuss."

"Yeah." Gar backed into the room and shut the door.

Damn. That gunslinger is awake and he's being careful. He's keeping a shotgun handy. Probably one of those double-barreled boomers that a man couldn't miss with if he tried. Damn.

CHAPTER 26

Bill Williams moved one careful step at a time now, carrying the powder keg. He started at the front door of the bunkhouse and backed up, pouring the black powder out onto the ground, stringing it out. Got to get it right next to the building. Hope there's enough. He put each foot down lightly as he backed around the corner to the rear of the building, still stringing out the powder. No back door. Good.

It took time, but eventually he had the building ringed with black powder, and he backed to the cattle chute where he'd left the rifle, stringing powder all the way. He couldn't tell how much was left, and he needed more. His job wasn't done.

It was farther to the main house, across ground that had been trampled bare of grass. To get there, he had to pass in front of the bunkhouse. Just thinking about being caught there without his rifle was scary. Gar and his scattergun would tear him in two. Bill squatted behind the cattle chute and worried about it.

Well, he wasn't going to leave the job half-done.

Not if he could help it. He stood and started across the yard, carrying what was left of the black powder. One step at a time, careful and ready to run. One at a time.

The quarter moon was an asset and a handicap. It showed him where to go, but it also made him a target if anyone happened to look out the bunkhouse window. A dim target, but a target. Slow. Careful. There. Now, the next step. Careful.

The main house was two-story, and the roof blocked out the

172

moon, creating a dark shadow. Bill breathed a sigh of relief when he finally reached the shadow. But still he had to move carefully. The front door faced the corrals and the bunkhouse, and was easy to find. He had to make his way around the house and find the back door, if there was one.

One slow step at a time—and he found it. He was on the moonlight side of the house now. Hugging the wall, he poured black powder under the back door and along the edge of the building. Only by feel could he tell how much powder he was pouring out. Now he had to cross the yard again, back across, pouring powder. Suddenly he froze.

The bunkhouse door was opening.

Bill stood perfectly still, knowing that if he moved he would be seen. Stood like an immovable object, like a bush or a fence post. He didn't dare even put the keg down and reach for his pistol.

"Hearin' things again, Gar?"

"Yeah, I got a feelin'." Gar stood in the door again.

"That Williams feller's got you spooked, Gar. Ain't nothin' out there, 'less it's that old Dandy horse. He's always snortin' at somethin'."

"I'm goin' out there and take a look."

"You can't see nothin' in the dark."

"I'm goin' out." The shadow in the door moved, moved toward Bill.

It was another time when Bill was afraid to breathe. If he drew his pistol, the movement would be seen and Gar would fire that shotgun. He wouldn't have to aim it, just point it in Bill's direction and bang away.

He had to chance it. Gar was coming right at him. Slowly, he started shifting the keg to his left arm.

"Goddammit, a man can't walk out here barefooted. Jesus Christ, I didn't know there was so goddamn many rocks." The shadow retreated and then appeared in the doorway. It disappeared inside.

Now he had to move fast. Gar would pull on his boots and be back. No time for catwalking. He turned the keg upside down and let the powder pour faster as he half-ran to the side of the bunkhouse.

Dropping the keg there, he turned and walked with rapid steps to the cattle chute.

"Hey, there is somebody out there. I hear somebody walkin', Gar. Where's that scattergun?"

"Can't get these goddamn boots on. Git out there. Shoot ever'thing that moves."

"It's that goddamn Williams. I'd bet anything it's him."

Bill was behind the chute now. He jerked a wooden match out of a shirt pocket, the same pocket that carried the letter to his brothers.

"See 'im?"

"Naw, but there's somebody out there."

He struck the match on the sole of his boot. It sputtered, flared and went out.

"Goddamn. There he is. Over by the chute. I seen a match."

Reached for another one. Nervous now. No longer cool. Hands shaking. Calm yourself, Bill Williams, he muttered. He struck it on the sole of his boot and cupped it in his hands until it was burning, then put it to the trail of black powder.

"Shoot, goddamnit."

A flame two feet high traveled down the crooked trail of black powder like a big snake, the biggest snake Bill had ever seen.

"Jesus Christ."

A shot boomed from the bunkhouse door. The slug *thunked* into a plank on the cattle chute. Bill had the Winchester to his shoulder. He fired at the shadow in the door, then dropped onto his stomach. The first shadow disappeared, but another appeared, and a boom like cannon-fire blasted the night. Splinters flew off the chute above Bill's head. If he had been standing or even kneeling he would have died right there.

Fire flared up in front of the bunkhouse as the flame reached more black powder. It quickly surrounded the house, lighting up the night.

"Jesus Christ."

A figure ran through the door and into the yard, running as fast as a man could run. Bill's rifle cracked, and the figure dropped. Another man ran out. Again the Winchester spoke. Three down. How many more?

174

Fire had reached the main house now, and the back of the house was bright red. Bill tried to watch both doors. There had to be more men in the bunkhouse.

A fourth man tried to run for it, going full tilt when he hit the yard. Crack, went the Winchester. The man hit the ground rolling, then lay still.

Two more men used better strategy. They came through the door together, firing six-guns as fast as they could cock the hammers and squeeze the triggers. Bullets hit the ground near Bill's face, hit the chute planks, whistled past his head.

Instinct told him to duck for cover, but his mind willed him to return the fire. Aim and shoot. He had the advantage. They were in the light of the house fire while he was in the dark. But only for a few seconds. Twice in rapid succession the Winchester barked. One man fell. The other got away in the black night.

It was getting dangerous now. That one man could sneak around behind him. But he couldn't leave yet. He waited, the rifle to his shoulder. The bunkhouse was going up in flames, but no more men were running out.

At the main house, the front door opened, and there he was, running into the yard, stumbling, rather, in his bare feet. He was wearing a long night shirt. Wouldn't you know the soft Eastern sonofabitch would wear something like that. He was waving his white fat hands and screaming like a terrified woman. Actually screaming.

There was no hesitation. A slug from the Winchester knocked the Dutchman's right leg from under him, and he fell to the ground, rolling and screaming. Crying.

"Pleass. Dond't shoot. Dond't shoot me. Pleass." He was on his knees now, begging. "Pleass."

Bill's lips curled in disgust as he aimed for the center of the soft face. "This is for Little Mouse," he muttered.

But a noise behind him shot a cold fear up his spine. Reacting instantly, he hit the ground flat and rolled. A bullet slammed into the ground where he'd been. He snapped a shot at the gunflash, jacked another shell into the Winchester and fired again. A grunt, and the sound of a man falling.

Bill rolled again and kept rolling until he was at the other end of the cattle chute. He jerked his eyes back to the houses and the ranch yard. The only man in sight who showed any life was the Dutchman, still on his knees, crying like a baby.

Flames climbed over most of the bunkhouse now, and the back of the main house was going up too. Bill waited, the rifle to his shoulder. No one else appeared.

Five bodies lay in the yard. One raised up on its knees, fell, raised up again, and started dragging itself. Bill aimed, but changed his mind. Whoever he was, he was only half-dressed, no pants or shirt and only one boot, and he had no gun. Bill watched, and finally stood.

If he was smart, he'd leave now. He'd done what he came to do. No, not quite. The Dutchman was still alive. Hurting and begging, but still alive. Bill carried the rifle in his left hand and kept the six-gun in his right hand, leveled and ready as he walked into the yard. Only two men appeared to be alive. One was still crawling. Bill went to him and recognized him immediately. Gar.

He could have kicked him in the head or shot him. Thinking of Little Mouse, he pointed the six-gun at the back of Gar's head. Gar looked up, recognized him too. He groaned, coughed blood and spoke in a strangling voice, "What're you gonna do, Williams? You gonna kill me while I'm not armed?"

Bill squatted beside him. "I'm gonna kill you the way you killed Little Mouse."

"Who?"

"The Indian woman at my camp."

"He told me to. I wouldn't of done it but he told me to." Gar coughed and more blood appeared around his mouth.

No use talking. Shoot the sonofabitch and get it over with. Gar coughed again and collapsed onto his face. Bill lowered the pistol, and, with his left hand, rolled Gar over. The bullet had hit him low in the stomach. Blood was matting the thick curly pubic hair. Gar drew his knees up and shuddered and groaned in pain. He wouldn't live another hour.

Feeling a little weak in the stomach himself now, Bill left Gar and went to the Dutchman. Aarnstadt was still on his knees with tears running down his face.

"Dond't shoot me. Pleass. I haf money. I haf a lodt uff money. I vill gif you a lodt uff money."

"I'll bet you have. Conglomerate money." Bill looked down at him. "Where? In the house?"

"Chess. I vill tell chew vere if chew dond't shoot me."

A dry chuckle came out of Bill as he looked up at the house. It was burning fast. "Won't the conglomerate be tickled when they find out some of their money went up in smoke."

"Pleass, dond't shoot me."

Bending down, Bill pushed the man over on his back. The right leg was badly broken with a shard of bone showing. "All right, you sonofabitch, I won't shoot you. If you live, you'll walk funny for the rest of your life and you won't stay in this territory." His lips curled in disgust again. "You ain't worth shooting."

A long look around, and Bill was satisfied. The bunkhouse was wrapped in flames and the main house soon would be. He was calm again. A little queasy in the stomach, but calm. He wasn't happy nor proud of himself. He'd done an unpleasant chore, one that had to be done. Gripping the Winchester in his left hand and the six-shooter in his right, he walked away toward his horses.

Lamplights on the streets of Colorado City were only pinpoints of brightness in the distance as Bill skirted the town. He kept to the south until he was on the other side, near where the Soda Springs were supposed to be. He looked up at the huge dark blob of mountains and turned north, searching for the Ute Trail.

It wasn't hard to find, even in the night. A wide, well-traveled wagon road, it led into a canyon and went sharply uphill deep into the mountains. Bill wondered how far it went, and if there were more trails where that one ended. Had to be. He'd follow them as far west as they went, maybe all the way to California.

Two miles up the trail, he stopped to let his horses blow. He had a terrible urge to turn in his saddle, but he ordered himself to look straight ahead. Finally, he touched spurs to the sorrel and went on.

No use looking back.

THE END

Be sure to check out the next novel in
Doyle Trent's Tales of the Old Wild West series:

CHEYENNE BROTHER

FROM WESTERN AUTHOR DOYLE TRENT
COMES THE AMERICAN FRONTIER SERIES

TALES OF THE OLD WILD WEST

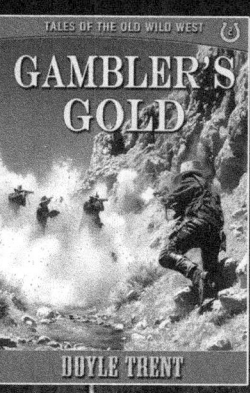

AND **24** ADDITIONAL TALES AWAIT

AVAILABLE IN PAPERBACK AND EBOOK

LOOKING FOR ACTION & ADVENTURE
AUTHOR ALAN CAILLOU
DELIVERS !

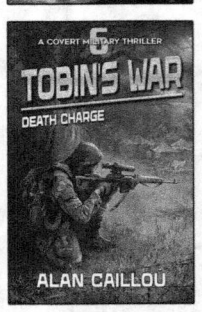

AVAILABLE IN PAPERBACK AND EBOOK

ADDITIONAL ACTION & ADVENTURE
FROM ALAN CAILLOU

AVAILABLE IN PAPERBACK AND EBOOK

CALIBERCOMICS.COM

DON'T MISS ANY OF MICHAEL KASNER'S
HARD HITTING MILITARY NOVEL SERIES

BLACK OPS

Formed by an elite cadre of government officials, the Black OPS team goes where the law can't - to seek retribution for acts of terror directed against Americans anywhere in the world.

3 BOOK SERIES

Armed with all the tactical advantages of modern technology, battle hard and ready when the free world is threatened - the Peacekeepers are the baddest grunts on the planet.

4 BOOK SERIES

CHOPPER COPS

America is being torn apart as criminal cartels terrorize our cities, dealing drugs and death wholesale. Local police are outgunned, so the President unleashes the U.S. TACTICAL POLICE FORCE. An elite army of super cops with ammo to burn, they swoop down on the hot spots in sleek high-tech attack choppers to win the dirty war and take back America!

4 BOOK SERIES

FROM CALIBER BOOKS

www.calibercomics.com

FROM FANTASY AND SCIENCE FICTION
AUTHOR ROLAND J. GREEN
THREE EPIC SERIES

FROM CALIBER BOOKS IN PAPERBACK AND EBOOK

DON'T MISS ANY OF NEIL HUNTER'S NOVELS FROM CALIBER BOOKS

Reporter Les Mason is completing an expose on the Long Point Nuclear Plant. But before he can finish he dies an agonizing death. The doctors are baffled—and there are similar cases to follow...Chris Lane, his girlfriend, and organizer of the Long Point Protestors, discovers Mason's notes, and decides to find out for herself what the plant has to hide.

2 BOOK SERIES

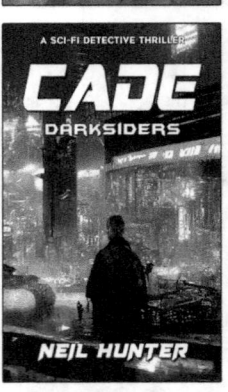

In middle of the 21st century America – over-populated decaying cities are ruled by hi-tech gangs pushing every vice and wastelands are controlled by bands of mutants. Ordinary citizens are oppressed and face a hopeless future. But Marshal T.J. Cade is a new breed of law enforcer. Teamed with his cyborg partner, Janek, Cade takes on these criminals and works in the gray areas of the law to get the job done.

3 BOOK SERIES

The village of Shepthorne England wasn't being gripped, but strangled by a winter's blanket of heavy snow and Arctic temperatures. The trouble began innocently enough with a massive pile-up of autos on frozen roads leading to and from the village. Then, from the sky, a military transport plane with its top secret cargo of devastation crashed down towards the center of the village. Hell was just beginning to touch Shepthorne and its unsuspecting citizens...

FROM CALIBER BOOKS  CALIBER BOOKS

www.calibercomics.com

CALIBER COMICS GOES TO WAR!
HISTORICAL AND MILITARY THEMED GRAPHIC NOVELS

**WORLD WAR ONE:
MO MAN'S LAND**

ISBN: 9781635298123

*A look at World War 1 from
the French trenches as they
faced the Imperial German
Army.*

**CORTEZ AND THE FALL
OF THE AZTECS**

ISBN: 9781635299779

*Cortez battles the Aztecs
while in search of Inca
gold.*

**TROY:
AN EMPIRE UNDER SIEGE**

ISBN: 9781635298635

*Homer's famous The Iliad and
the Trojan War is given a
unique human perspective
rather than from the God's.*

WITNESS TO WAR

ISBN: 9781635299700

*WW2's Battle of the Bulge
is seen up close by an
embedded female war
reporter.*

THE LINCOLN BRIGADE

ISBN: 9781635298222

*American volunteers head
to Spain in the 1930s to
fight in their civil war
against the fascist regime.*

**EL CID:
THE CONQUEROR**

ISBN: 9780982654996

*Europe's greatest warrior
attempts to unify Spain
against invading foreign
and domestic armies.*

WINTER WAR

ISBN: 9780985749392

*At the outbreak of WW2
Finland fights against an
invading Soviet army.*

**ZULUNATION:
END OF EMPIRE**

ISBN: 9780941613415

*The global British Empire
and far-reaching influence
is threatened by a Zulu
uprising in southern Africa.*

AIR WARRIORS: WORLD WAR ONE #V1 - V4   *Take to the skies of WW1 as various fighter aces tell their harrowing stories.*
ISBN: 9781635297973 (V1), 9781635297980 (V2), 9781635297997 (V3), 9781635298000 (V4)

CALIBER COMICS GOES TO THE EDGE!
Science Fiction and Horror themed graphic novels

DEADWORLD
ISBN: 9781942351245

RENFIELD
ISBN: 9781942351825

NOSFERATU
ISBN: 9781942351931

**LOVECRAFT:
THE EARLY STORIES**
ISBN: 9781942351634

**THE WAR OF THE WORLDS:
INFESTATION**
ISBN: 9781942351962

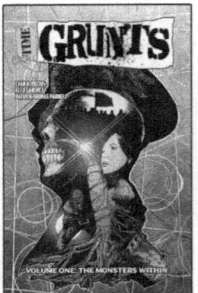

TIME GRUNTS
ISBN: 9781635299472

DRACULA
ISBN: 9780996030649

**DRACULA:
THE SUICIDE CLUB**
ISBN: 9781635299571

**JACK THE RIPPER
ILLUSTRATED**
ISBN: 9781942351917

THE SEARCHERS
ISBN: 9781942351979

A.A.I. WARS
ISBN: 9781635299168

**AUTUMN: TERROR IN THE
LONDON UNDERGROUND**
ISBN: 9781544624020

www.calibercomics.com

ALSO AVAILABLE FROM CALIBER COMICS

QUALITY GRAPHIC NOVELS TO ENTERTAIN

THE SEARCHERS: VOLUME 1
The Shape of Things to Come

Before *League of Extraordinary Gentlemen* there was *The Searchers*. At the dawn of the 20th Century the greatest literary adventurers from the minds of Wells, Doyle, Burroughs, and Haggard were created. All thought to be the work of pure fiction. However, a century later, the real-life descendents of those famous characters are recuited by the legendary Professor Challenger in order to save mankind's future. Series collected for the first time.

"Searchers is the comic book I have on the wall with a sign reading - 'Love books? Never read a comic? Try this one! ....money back guarantee..." - Dark Star Books.

WAR OF THE WORLDS: INFESTATION

Based on the H.G. Wells classic! The "Martian Invasion" has begun again and now mankind must fight for its very humanity. It happened slowly at first but by the third year, it seemed that the war was almost over... the war was almost lost.

"Writer Randy Zimmerman has a fine grasp of drama, and spins the various strands of the story into a coherent whole... imaginative and very gritty."
- war-of-the-worlds.co.uk

HELSING: LEGACY BORN

From writer Gary Reed (Deadworld) and artists John Lowe (Captain America), Bruce McCorkindale (Godzilla). She was born into a legacy she wanted no part of and pushed into a battle recessed deep in the shadows of the night. Samantha Helsing is torn between two worlds...two allegiances...two families. The legacy of the Van Helsing family and their crusade against the "night creatures" comes to modern day with the most unlikely of all warriors.

"Congratulations on this masterpiece..."
- Paul Dale Roberts, Compuserve Reviews

DEADWORLD

Before there was The Walking Dead there was Deadworld. Here is an introduction of the long running classic horror series, Deadworld, to a new audience! Considered by many to be the godfather of the original zombie comic with over 100 issues and graphic novels in print and over 1,000,000 copies sold, Deadworld ripped into the undead with intelligent zombies on a mission and a group of poor teens riding in a school bus desperately try to stay one step ahead of the sadistic, Harley-riding King Zombie. Death, mayhem, and a touch of supernatural evil made Deadworld a classic and now here's your chance to get into the story!

DAYS OF WRATH

Award winning comic writer & artist Wayne Vansant brings his gripping World War II saga of war in the Pacific to Guadalcanal and the Battle of Bloody Ridge. This is the powerful story of the long, vicious battle for Guadalcanal that occurred in 1942-43. When the U.S. Navy orders its outnumbered and out-gunned ships to run from the Japanese fleet, they abandon American troops on a bloody, battered island in the South Pacific.

"Heavy on authenticity, compellingly written and beautifully drawn."
- Comics Buyers Guide

SHERLOCK HOLMES:
THE CASE OF THE MISSING MARTIAN

Sherlock is called out of retirement to London in 1908 to solve a most baffling mystery: The British Museum is missing a specimen of a Martian from the failed invasion of 1899. Did it walk away on its own or did someone steal it?

Holmes remembers the facts and remembers his part in the war effort alongside Professor Challenger during the War of the Worlds invasion that was chronicled in H.G. Wells' classic novel.

Meanwhile, Doctor Watson has problems of his own when his wife steals a scalpel from his surgical tool kit and returns to her old stomping grounds of Whitechapel, the London

CALIBER PRESENTS

The original Caliber Presents anthology title was one of Caliber's inaugural releases and featured predominantly new creators, many of which went onto successful careers in the comics' industry. In this new version, Caliber Presents has expanded to graphic novel size and while still featuring new creators it also includes many established professional creators with new visions. Creators featured in this first issue include nominees and winners of some of the industry's major awards including the Eisner, Harvey, Xeric, Ghastly, Shel Dorf, Comic Monsters, and more.

LEGENDLORE

From Caliber Comics now comes the entire Realm and Legendlore saga as a set of volumes that collects the long running critically acclaimed series. In the vein of The Lord of The Rings and The Hobbit with elements of Game of Thrones and Dungeon and Dragons.

Four normal modern day teenagers are plunged into a world they thought only existed in novels and film. They are whisked away to a magical land where dragons roam the skies, orcs and hobgoblins terrorize travelers, where unicorns prance through the forest, and kingdoms wage war for dominance. It is a world where man is just one race, joining other races such as elves, trolls, dwarves, changelings, and the dreaded night creatures who steal the night.

TIME GRUNTS

What if Hitler's last great Super Weapon was – Time itself! A WWII/time travel adventure that can best be described as *Band of Brothers* meets *Time Bandits*.

October, 1944. Nazi fortunes appear bleaker by the day. But in the bowels of the Wenceslas Mines, a terrible threat has emerged . . . The Nazis have discovered the ability to conquer time itself with the help of a new ominous device!

Now a rag tag group of American GIs must stop this threat to the past, present, and future . . . While dealing with their own past, prejudices, and fears in the process.

CALIBER
COMICS

www.calibercomics.com

www.ingramcontent.com/pod-product-compliance
Lightning Source LLC
Chambersburg PA
CBHW051513170626
46811CB00002B/800